Cooking Up Christmas

CS Jane

For my Nanny

Chapter 1

A hand in the air, raised high over her head, determined to get a taxi, Tessa tapped the pointed front of her expensive high heel against the pavement. The location of her job's building, near Rockefeller Center, made it nearly impossible to do most things in the month of December—getting a taxi was high on that list. Her apartment was all the way downtown and felt like continents away after a long day entertaining existing clients and weaving together perfectly-pitched advertising campaigns to lock in new ones. She loved living in New York City, but it was nights like this that the holiday hubbub made it more than exhausting.

"Come on!" she yelled out loud as yellow car after yellow car whizzed past, leaving her to fend for herself on the crowded sidewalks, bustling with holiday shoppers and tourists. Each person pushed harder than the next to make their way toward the renowned Christmas tree that filled the square at *Thirty Rock* with thousands of twinkling lights and unimaginable crowds.

Finally, a cab slammed to a stop at the curb, kicking up brown, over-salted snow and muck across her knee-length designer jacket. Looking down at the droplets that sprinkled her chest, she took an exaggerated breath before pulling the door open and slipping into the backseat of the cab.

"Bleecker and sixth," she said as she fumbled through her bag in search of her cell phone.

"Ya gonna say please? It is the holiday season after all," the cab driver mumbled.

She rolled her eyes and looked up to meet his gaze on her in the rearview mirror, and said, "Please and thank you."

The cab jolted to a start, only to slam on its breaks moments later to avoid hitting starry-eyed pedestrians, too captivated by the magic of Christmas in the big city to look both ways before crossing the street.

Tessa always wanted to live in New York City, and she enjoyed it eleven months out of the year. But December was not one of them. Between the tourists and holiday specials, December felt like a constant intrusion on her personal space, making it impossible to consider getting in the holiday spirit herself.

As she scrolled through her e-mails, already piling up in her inbox despite leaving the office just twenty minutes ago, she wondered what kind of jobs the people filling the sidewalks had that allowed them to spend their December's traipsing through the city to look at Christmas lights. Her own job barely offered her enough time to sleep, let alone spare a second for something as leisurely as a holiday stroll. She didn't have the time to put up and decorate a Christmas tree in her own home, and she would never dream of making her way to a crowded city to snap a selfie in front of its tree.

As she looked over her e-mails, a text message from her mom popped across the screen.

Dinner this weekend? It's been a while, T. Miss you.

Tessa loved her mom—would consider them to have been close at one time—but she wished she would understand that driving almost two hours out to the pinpoint of a town in the country where she grew up was the last thing she wanted to do on her weekends. Tessa left Chestnut Ridge over ten years ago at eighteen, with a plan to go back as little as possible, and mostly she had stuck to it. Pulling off her gloves, she tapped the text box on her phone, typing out one of her typical excuses—a work event or maintenance visit at her apartment—and returned to reading her e-mails.

"Did you get to see the tree yet?" the gray-haired cab driver asked. "It really is quite something, don't ya think? I like to walk by it as much as I can to take it all in."

If only he knew her thoughts. Tessa never wanted to come off as pretentious, but she hated making small talk with people when she didn't have to. She spent most of her day talking, either to clients or her own team. On a rare occasion when she didn't have to speak, she preferred a bit of quiet over chitchat. And clearly, her and the cab driver had varying opinions on fun. What kind of person preferred to walk through the hectic crowds drawn to the area near that Christmas tree?

"I don't really care to see it. It's the same every year," she said without looking up from her phone.

"Ah!" he said excitedly, causing her to lift from the seat. "You gotta go see the tree! You gotta do all the holiday stuff in the city, every year. The carriage ride through Central Park, that toy shop . . . What's it called?"

"I'm not sure what toy shop you're referring to," she mumbled.

"Eh, you know the one I mean." She did know—the one on the edge of the park—but she wasn't going to tell him. Not that he paused for her response. "And you can't forget the ice skating! It's what the magic of Christmas is all about. There's nothing better than Christmas in New York."

She could think of many things.

Looking back up into the mirror, she said, "There's nothing magical to it. Christmas is about major brands exploiting consumers into thinking we need to provide the perfect gift, the perfect meal, and have the perfect family. They make us believe everything needs to be perfect for the holidays, at the expense of our wallets and credit cards. Christmas is about profit margins, not magic."

"Bah!" he yelled, though she was happy he didn't add a *humbug.*

Her phone buzzed again with another message—a sad face emoji. Her mom just learned how to use the emoji keyboard and was now treading into the area of overuse. Every message came with a colorful cartoon at the end.

Sorry Mom, it's a crazy time of year. Maybe another time. Though she knew it probably wouldn't be anytime soon. She couldn't remember the last time she went out to visit.

Looking at her other messages, she clicked on one from Liam, a client whom she was semi-secretly and casually dating. If you count five dinner dates as seeing someone.

Drinks tonight?

Rubbing her temples, she could feel the tension building up behind her eyes for a massive headache. She could use a drink but didn't want to go back out on this wet night, too frustrated with the hassle of moving about. Not to mention she was trying to keep their dates to a strict once-per-week schedule so it wouldn't get too serious. She didn't have time to dedicate to anything more than that. After typing a response similar to the one she'd sent her mom, she closed her eyes, took in a breath, and sat that way, breathing slow to keep calm, until the cab pulled up in front of her apartment building.

"Home sweet home!" the driver said. "And a *very* Merry Christmas to you!" His head spun back to face her with a smile.

"You too," she said as she gathered her things and handed over a twenty before racing past the doorman into her building's entranceway. Her mom insisted that she live in a building with a doorman for an extra layer of safety, yet she'd never seen him stop anyone at the door.

Once in the elevator, she leaned against the far wall, blowing the stray hairs from her face. Her feet were throbbing, having spent the day tucked into heels and mostly standing. Looking in the reflection of the elevator doors, she appeared as run-down as she felt. She had secured herself on the fast track to success early on in her career, always being available for long hours or last-minute projects. While most would call her a workaholic, she preferred to consider herself driven. For years, she'd sacrificed things others valued—vacations, time with friends, a real relationship. But it was worth it.

Tessa pushed open the door to her apartment and was greeted by the soft drone of the radiator and her neutral-toned décor. After changing into comfier clothes, she made herself a quick salad of arugula and tomatoes, which hardly passed as dinner, then set up on the couch with her laptop and a glass of wine. Mindless television hummed in the background. She had to put the final touches on a presentation for a holiday campaign for the large, national jewelry brand Jay's Jewelers she'd been working on for most of the week. Even if the client approved her proposal in tomorrow's meeting, she would have just enough time to organize the creative before the three-day blast they were planning to lead up to the Christmas holiday. Though it was certainly last minute, Jay's was a long-standing client at the firm, and having extra advertising dollars to spend at the end of the year was too good of an opportunity to pass on.

Her phone buzzed on the coffee table, and she reached over to grab it. Frowning, she felt a ping of guilt. Her mother usually gave up more easily than this.

It's been months since I've seen you. How much maintenance could there be that needs to get done on that place? Can you please make the time? I'd love to see you, Tess.

She quickly typed out a plausible explanation and continued working on her laptop when her phone rang, showing an incoming call from her mother.

Sighing, she picked up the call. "Hi, Mom. Sorry, I'm just so swamped these days—you know how this time of year is for me. I barely have had a second to breathe."

"Oh, well I'm fine, Tessa, thank you for asking," her mother said, only half joking, a touch of sarcasm to her tone.

"Sorry, Mom. How are things?" Tessa pushed her laptop to the side to be able to reach her wine glass.

"Things are okay, other than the fact that I haven't seen my only daughter in almost a year."

After a long sip, she said, "That's not true, we met for coffee that one time recently."

"A ten-minute coffee break doesn't count as spending time with you, sweetie, not to mention that was still in the beginning of

14

May. It's December, if you haven't noticed by the snow on the ground and the Christmas decorations around you. Or are you too busy for all that too?" Her mom would be heartbroken to know there were zero decorations on display in her apartment—not a smidgen of red or green could be found.

"Oh, I've noticed," Tessa said sarcastically. "Between that and the tourists, the city has been an absolute nightmare."

"Well then, that gives you an even better reason to come home for Christmas."

Tessa tried to hide the frustration building in her tone. "You know I don't get time off, aside from Christmas Day, and that's hardly enough time to come all the way out to Chestnut Ridge." This was not entirely true. She was one of the lucky few whose company closed for the week in between Christmas and New Year's Day, but she had maintained this point with her mom since moving to the city and wasn't about to cave on it now.

"Come on, Tess. We both know you have the time off. It'll be fun! Just like old times—me and you and your Nana here in spirit. We could do all the same Christmas traditions we used to. Get the tree, put out the nutcrackers, bake all the different kinds of cookies. I even found her old cookbook, the one she wrote all her holiday recipes in. We could cook them all, Tess, and have a Christmas Eve feast like we used to back in the day!"

Perhaps it was the wine, but Tessa's eyes began to sting at their corners as she thought about her childhood back home with her mom and Nana. It had just been the three of them—she never knew her father, and her grandfather died when she was too young to remember. "I don't think I can make it, Mom. I'm sorry, I really am. And anyways, you know that I'm horrible in the kitchen. I could never cook like Nana. You'll have more fun without me, trust me."

"Will you think about it, Tess? Please? For me? I don't care if you're a nightmare in the kitchen, I just want to spend some time with you."

16

Not knowing what else to say, she agreed that she would think about it, told her mom she loved her, and hung up the phone. She would come up with a better reason as it got closer, but for now, she needed to finish this presentation and close her deal with Jay's. Securing additional business at the year's end was the best way to ensure a larger Christmas bonus.

One more glass of wine later, Tessa realized it was well past midnight and the pulsing in her strained eyes was becoming hard to ignore. Scrolling through her part of the presentation one last time, she closed her laptop and stood, ready to fall into bed for a few hours of desperately-needed rest.

Though she was tired, she could already tell that she wouldn't be able to sleep. Why her bed always seemed immensely more comfortable in the morning than at night, she would never know. Looking back at her cell phone, Tessa skimmed over the conversation with her mom and was saddened by the way she could tell her daughter was avoiding her and Chestnut Ridge. It really had been a long time since she'd gone back home, but there was just too much there that she was excited to leave. When she shut the door on her life and who she was in that town, she had hoped it would be forever. Not that there was anything that bad to run from—she had a lovely childhood, idyllic even. It was just that, from a young age she knew she wanted more out of life than what that town could offer. Since she could remember, she saw herself glowing under the city lights, making something of her life—not back home in a town that only had one traffic light.

If she was being honest with herself, though, her mother and Nana had become victims of her fleeing her hometown. Even before her Nana died, she had returned very few times to see her, which was something she'd come to regret mere seconds after learning of her passing.

She clicked into her phone's photo stream and scrolled back to the one she kept from when she was younger. Before she left for college, while packing up her room, she had taken a photo on her cell phone of the old, faded snapshot she kept in her desk drawer. There Tessa was, standing on a stool, each arm around her mom and nana, a battered wooden spoon in her hand and her oversized smock of an apron covered in flour. Plates of freshly-baked cookies piled high on the table in front of them, all three of their proud smiles beaming as bright as that darned Christmas tree in the city.

Tessa could remember that day like it was yesterday, could still smell the batch of peanut butter blossoms baking in the oven when the photo was taken. She had gotten a new clunky camera as an early gift, probably an inappropriate gift for how old she was at the time, but she loved it. She had looked through the lens from every angle trying to find the perfect place to prop the camera so she could snap the shot of the three of them. Her Nana was impressed that she not only knew how to use the camera but that she could also set the timer so they could all be in the photo. Proudly, she had exclaimed, "You're such a smarty, my little petunia!" It was a pet name she had started calling Tessa when she was just days old. "Would you just look at what the world has come up with? Who would've thought—a self-taking camera! Back in my day, someone actually had to press the button."

Tessa loved how impressed her Nana was by new technology. Though most of the time she couldn't learn to use it herself, she would ask questions and would want to know every detail of how something worked, only to laugh it off and say how lucky kids were today and that she couldn't have dreamed of all the things Tessa had. Her Nana was the definition of old-school, and she was the only person Tessa knew who never used a microwave and joyfully spent hours in the kitchen making everything from scratch. She never minded the work and swore it was not worth sacrificing the quality of her food for just a few extra seconds of her day. Whether that was the secret or not, no one cooked food that tasted as good as her Nana's.

Wiping away a single tear that slipped from her eye, she closed the phone and placed it back on her bedside table. It was almost three in the morning, and she desperately needed to sleep as her alarm would be ringing in just a few short hours. Rolling onto her side, she closed her eyes and thought about all the delicious recipes that lived within her Nana's handwritten Christmas recipe book and like a child, she fell asleep, her stomach growling and her mind full of sweet memories and treats from her past.

Chapter 2

"I just feel like it's off—completely misses the mark on what we were looking for. We want to pull at last minute shoppers' heartstrings, appeal to them to open their wallets. This—this type of campaign won't even turn heads. There's nothing special here."

Tessa's throat instantly dried out as she struggled to swallow. She glanced around the conference room table at Ben, her boss and superior, for guidance on how to respond.

When he offered nothing, she said, "Well let's chat about it then. Maybe we can identify where we are off. I'm sure after a small brainstorm we can correct any issues you have with the campaign."

"Christmas is coming up fast. We said we needed to hit it out of the park, move quickly, and now you're recommending a brainstorm session? Based on what I see here, I'd say we've missed the boat."

Tessa smiled as she learned to do long ago with angry clients and again glanced over at Ben who finally jumped in to defend the vision of the presentation and remind the client of the tight deadline. Normally, Ben could sell anything to the client but this one, Jay's Jewelers, seemed to only be getting more frustrated at each of his attempts.

"Do you people even celebrate Christmas? I questioned the lack of red and green in the office and the fact that there was zero holiday cheer, but I was certain an experienced firm such as yourselves could manage a last-minute holiday advertising campaign."

Tessa's attention snapped back to the table. "Of course we do," she said, mildly convincing. "We all love Christmas around here. My assistant, Andy, you should see her, she's bursting at the seams with holiday cheer."

"Really? Tell me then, what does Christmas mean to you? What brings the twinkle to your eye? When you think about the joy and love of Christmas, what do you think about?"

Tessa was eager to seal the deal, and she was relying on the fact that the client sitting with her was a retailer. "Presents, of course. The idea of waking up and being gifted something beautiful and exquisite from someone special."

Jay himself simply nodded his head slowly, clearly disappointed. "And that, my dear, seems to be exactly the problem. You're not diving deep enough into the true meaning of Christmas, but are approaching this in a shallow way. It's not about the gifts, you see. It's about the thought and feeling behind the gift. The fact that someone you love went out and spent the time, chose something specifically for you. They decided to buy that piece of jewelry because it made them feel like it was the perfect item to put under your tree. It could be anything in the box, any style or at any price point, but it's the gesture that counts. And you, Tessa, do not capture that magic here. This campaign you're presenting is as cold and bland as snow."

Her ears hissed as she opened her mouth to speak, but she was cut off by Ben as he apologized for being off base and promised they would rework the creative concept. But Jay was already standing to leave the room.

"We've been with this firm since the beginning of Jay's," he said looking to Ben. "Our fathers partnered and turned a one-shop jewelry store into a nationally recognized brand and I don't want to make any impulsive decisions today, but I am going to have to think a bit about our partnership in the future. I have a nagging feeling that with us being your largest client and floating the firm's bills that the work here has become quite"—he looked over at Tessa, who was now standing—"uninspired."

He turned to leave but stopped, nearly bumping into Ben who was chasing behind him. "Christmas campaigns should be bursting with heart. Family, love, tradition . . . It's the only time of year a car or candy commercial and their recognizable jingles can pause a distracted audience in their tracks and make them smile. You see that big red bow on the hood of the car and hear that music, and it just feels like the holidays. This . . ." he said, holding up the proposal she worked hours on. "This feels fake. Forced even. You needed to capture the magic of Christmas but I'm not even sure you know what that is." Jay nodded before exiting the room, Ben on his heels, trying desperately to repair the damage. Not securing the extra dollars for this campaign is disappointing, but losing Jay's Jewelers as a client would be devastating to the firm and she didn't know an advertising agency in the city that wanted to lose their biggest client heading into the new year.

Alone in the conference room, Tessa let out an exasperated sigh. Flipping through the proposal in front of her, she wondered how she could have been so off with her recommendations? Sitting back at the table, she knew better than to leave the conference room. Ben would be back soon, ready to rehash everything that went wrong and ream into her about the concept that he himself had approved. She looked down at her phone, clicked back into her saved photos, and stared down on that snapshot of her and her mom and Nana. Was Jay right? Had she lost the magic of Christmas? She hadn't even gone home for the holidays since her nana passed three years ago.

"Well that was a disaster, Tess." Ben said, interrupting her thoughts.

"I know, and I'm sorry. I thought it was on target. He said he wanted to sell more earring and necklace sets, and I thought we hit on that goal." She pointed down at the presentation where jewelry sets were clearly highlighted.

"How long have you worked here?" Ben continued, without taking a seat at the table.

"Since I interned here in college, so what's that now? Eight years or so?" Tessa didn't like the tone of the conversation and nervously tapped her pen against the table. "I know I messed up, but you know I've given my heart and soul to this firm. I will work harder, make it up . . ."

"I'm concerned that's the point, Tess. You're always here. You don't take breaks. You're the only one on my payroll who doesn't beg to use weeks of their paid time off during the holidays. Have you even gone home for Christmas since working here? I don't think I've ever heard anything about your family."

"I take breaks. I go out for lunch a few times a week, Ben."

"I'm not talking about work lunch with clients. You never use your time off, and the only person I've seen you date is Liam. And yes, I know about that and can't say I completely understand your motives there."

Tessa opened her mouth to talk, but Ben interrupted her. "You said it yourself—you've given your heart to this job. As your employer I shouldn't be complaining, and I wouldn't be, except that we just had a very unsuccessful meeting with our biggest client because he could feel that in your work. And I can't have clients leaving here questioning if we can deliver the Christmas magic, or any magic for that matter. We're an advertising firm, for goodness sake."

Tessa stood and placed both hands firmly on the edge of the conference room table. "Ben, I messed up, I'm sorry. Let me make it up to you. I will work through the night and come up with a completely new concept that Jay will love. I promise."

Ben shook his head. "No, Tess, that's not what I want right now. I want you to go home for Christmas and take some time with your family. Go back to that small town you came from and see your loved ones."

"That's ridiculous, Ben! What boss asks you to take time off during the holidays?"

Ben sighed. "This boss does. I can't have 'cold' on my creative team, Tess. You need to get back the magic, and home seems like a good place to start. Go spend some time with your family."

"Ben, Christmas is just one part of the year. All my other campaigns are spot on, and you know that. I'm your top performer—have been for years!"

"It'll be good for you, Tessa. Trust me. Get out of this city, go home."

Tessa couldn't hide her frustration. "If I wanted to go home to that small town, don't you think I'd be one of the people submitting for the time off, Ben? There's no magic to be found there—Christmas or any other kind."

"Then fly down to the Bahamas. I don't care what you do. But after this week, you are on a way overdue vacation until the new year. I will put it through the system with human resources." Walking away he yelled over his shoulder, "And Tess? No e-mail. I want to see your autoreply on, and I don't want to see a single note come through from your e-mail address—not even a holiday e-card." He smiled and said, "You have a very, Merry Christmas, Tess." And with a wink, he turned and walked out of the room.

"Ugh!" Tessa yelled, concerned very little with the glass walls of the room and the looks of the lower level employees as they stared back at her outburst.

"What?" she asked, as the assistants switched their glances back down to their computers. Gathering her notebook and files, she stomped down the hall to her office, her heels clicking every step of the way.

Back at her desk she put her head in her hands and took a few deep breaths before beginning to talk herself off the ledge. "This isn't permanent. You didn't get fired. This is just a forced vacation . . . Ugh! A forced vacation—that sounds like I'm getting fired. What am I going to do?"

"Knock knock!" Andy, her peppy young assistant popped her head in the door. "How'd it go?"

Tessa only had to look up at her for her to know.

"Eek! That bad, huh? Sorry to hear that. If you ask me, Jay is getting harder and harder to please. Really making everyone work for the hefty retainer. I heard that Ben followed him out like a puppy . . ."

Rubbing her temples, Tessa said, "Did you need something, Andy?"

"Ah, yes! Sorry. Ben told me to process your paid time off for the last two weeks of December, but I wanted to confirm with you first. You never go anywhere! Are you going someplace fun? How exciting! I love travelling—who doesn't?"

Tessa would not have thought she was old at thirty, but her twenty-two-year-old assistant had a way of constantly reminding her of their age difference. "I'm not going anywhere. Ben's making me take the time . . . says I need a break."

Andy rushed over to the chair and sat, leaning in closer. "Yikes, that doesn't sound good. Are you, like, freaking out right now? Cause I would totally be freaking out if Ben told me to take a break. If there's one thing I've learned from dating, a break is never good."

"It's not like that, Andy, I just never used my days and apparently, the company is starting a new push for work-life balance," she lied. "They want everyone to use a certain percentage of their paid time off before the end of the year."

Andy leaned back and put both hands up in the air. "Thank goodness, because I really like working for you and I did not need that type of news right before Christmas! It would have completely ruined my holiday cheer to have to get to know a new boss. I mean, not that you're easy or anything, but at least I know what it's like working for you."

Tessa rolled her eyes. "Well, I am thrilled I didn't ruin your cheer. Go ahead and process the time. I don't need Ben getting his pants all in a bunch."

Andy stood and bounced back toward the door. "Bummer! That means you won't be here for Secret Santa! Don't worry, I'll make the exchange for you and leave your gift on your desk for when you get back. I heard you might be getting something super fun!" She winked.

It was the least of her worries, but she thanked Andy and asked her to shut the door behind her when she left.

Twenty minutes later, as she bit into her organic granola bar, she couldn't find a single destination on the travel site she was searching that did not cost an astronomical amount. She looked everywhere. Out west, the Caribbean—there wasn't a single destination that was reasonable enough for her to pull out her credit card. The holiday season wasn't exactly the best time for last-minute travel deals.

Clicking over from the travel site to her e-mail, she saw an unopened message from Liam.

Wish we met up last night ☹ I wanted to tell you in person, but I'm heading out of town for a few weeks. Sorry to leave you alone for the holiday, but I'm sure you're swamped anyways. Don't be mad, I'll see you in the new year! ☺

"That's just great," she said out loud to herself. She knew that she and Liam were dating casually, but she'd have thought he'd at least have felt the need to tell her where he was heading. Or give her a call for that matter . . . not send a short e-mail with two emojis. Going back over the e-mail, her blood rushed to her face as she reread his message, more annoyed the second time.

Her phone vibrated on her desk, and she reached to pick it up without moving her eyes from the screen.

"This is Tessa."

"Oh, hi, sweetie! I didn't think you'd pick up midday! I had the script for my guilt-filled voicemail all planned out already!" Her mom chuckled.

"I always try to answer your calls, Mom. Sometimes I'm just busy," Tessa said, knowing it was only part of the truth.

"Please, spare me!" Her mom said with an exaggerated laugh.

Swiveling in her chair, she swung back to face the glass window that looked out into the office space. As her mom continued chatting about how she thought it would do Tessa good to relax around the holidays, she watched the other coworkers happily interact with each other on the other side of the glass, clearly smitten with the joy of the season. She knew Andy had carols performed by pop singers playing from her computer speakers, and that Jonathan was scanning the internet for the perfect gifts for his wife. Each year all the women would lean on his desk, exclaiming in a mix of oohs and aahs and swooning about how sweet his gifts were. Jan, one of the older executive assistants, already dropped off her personalized Christmas cards with a tin of treats for each of the employees, and all the interns were thrilled with the added snacks in the lunch room from clients and vendors. Christmas was, in fact, all around her, yet maybe Jay was partially right—she hadn't paid attention to it in years. Long ago she was a girl who was ecstatic over the holidays. She'd spend the entire month involved in one holiday activity or another, and here she was now—older and being forced to take a vacation because she had grown cold.

"Are you even listening to me at all, T? I'm trying to talk to you, and I can tell you're doing work on your computer instead of listening." It wasn't the first time her mom had caught her not giving all of her attention.

"Sorry Mom, I didn't mean to. I was actually going to call you tonight about that."

"Oh yeah, everything alright?" She tried not to let it bother her that her mom sounded shocked.

"Yes, fine. I just wanted to tell you that I decided I would be coming home this year for Christmas after all."

Her mom squealed, and she knew she was dancing about her kitchen. "That is the best news, sweetheart. This is going to be so much fun! Why the change of heart? Not that I'm complaining, but I am curious!"

For some reason, she didn't want to tell her mom that she was practically being forced out of the office and that she messed up at work and was accused of not understanding the magic of Christmas. Somehow it made her feel like she was using her mom, and she didn't want her to feel that way.

"Just some policy change at work. Apparently to encourage work-life balance they want everyone to use there paid time off by the end of the year. So, I have the time now," she lied again.

"This is the best news! I am so excited, and now, my goodness, I have so much to do! When can I expect you in town? I hope at least for Christmas Eve—you know that has always been our favorite day of the year!"

Tessa debated telling her mom she would be coming just for the holiday but was afraid to get caught in her lie, so she settled for the truth. "Well, it turns out I have more time off than I thought. I have two weeks, so if it's alright with you I'll be coming this weekend."

Her mom shrieked even louder than the first time. "What a Christmas miracle! My baby home in my house for two weeks! This is going to be so much fun, Tess, I know it. I'm too excited to think right now, but we can do it all like we used to!"

"Well, I am really looking forward to it." And she was.

"Thank you, Tess. This really means a lot to me."

"I know, Mom, me too."

After a few more planning details, her mom hung up the phone, exclaiming she had so much to do now that they had their special girl time planned. She listed off an extensive list of preparations, which Tessa insisted wasn't necessary, knowing well enough her mom would do it all anyway.

After hanging up the phone, Tessa felt bad that she wasn't as excited as her mother to go back to Chestnut Ridge. Not that it had anything to do with her mom—she loved her and only ever wanted the best for her. It was just that small town, and how its residents knew everyone and their business.

And him—there was always him. Chase, her high school boyfriend she'd run away from years earlier. The love of her life whom no man has been able to replace. The social media profile she'd find herself on after a few glasses of wine, searching to see if he had settled down, always happy and relieved to see that he hadn't. Sighing, she scrolled through the remaining e-mails in her inbox, feeling less enthused than before to answer them. No use getting into anything new if she was going to be out of the office for two weeks with an autoreply on. With nothing else to do, she opened her Facebook page and typed in his name before quickly x-ing out of the browser, leaving only her e-mail open. Looks like she was heading back to Chestnut Ridge, New Jersey, for Christmas, and she didn't need to stir up any suppressed feelings about Chase.

As she scrolled aimlessly through her inbox, clicking from one holiday promotion to the next, she realized she hadn't gotten a chance to shop yet for a gift for her mom. In the years she didn't make it home, she'd send a large box filled with typical women's gifts. Usually some type of clothing item or accessory, perfume or a handbag. Her mom loved to read, so she'd throw in a few paperbacks and a pair of slippers and ship it off to Chestnut Ridge, content with her choices and happy to check it off her to-do list.

Realizing she couldn't go home empty-handed, she packed up the few items she would need from her desk and wrapped herself in her long coat and scarf. New York winters could be biting, and the current cold spell felt particularly harsh.

With one last look around her office, she closed the door behind her and let Andy know she would be leaving for the day.

"Wait!" she said, swinging her chair and popping to her feet. "I won't see you until after the holiday!" Andy extended both arms outward, a beaming smile plastered to her face. "Merry Christmas, Tessa!"

Tessa leaned in for a bottom-out hug as Andy squeezed her shoulders and rocked back and forth. "Merry Christmas to you too." With a wave to a few of her other coworkers, she purposely put her head down as she passed Ben's office and entered the elevator.

Once out on the street, she looked up and down sixth avenue trying to determine the closest store where she could shop for a gift. Her best bet would be the department store on 34th street, so she waited on the curb for a taxi before deciding to walk the fifteen blocks. Though it was cold, she could use the time to unwind, wrap her head around what just happened and what she'd just agreed to.

The city was certainly alive with the spirit of Christmas. The sidewalks sang their songs to the tune of people dressed up as Santa ringing bells, and each storefront window was adorned with elaborate displays that looked to be from a child's holiday dreams. For an already bright city, additional lights were strung from every available corner, and the people filling the streets were all buzzing from checking off items on their own to-do lists.

When she reached the department store, she looked up at the flawlessly-arranged red ribbon, wreaths, and lights that welcomed you to the storefront. Briefly, she felt the magic in the air, only to be brought back to the gritty sidewalk when someone bumped into her shoulder, sending her tripping into the revolving doors. It was a simple reminder that she had always loved

Christmas, but in New York, it only made her life more difficult and crowded.

As she weaved through the shoppers and different displays, a peppy saleswoman approached her. "Need help finding what you're looking for?"

Tessa waved her off, but noticed that the woman hung back and continued to follow her through the aisles of the store. As she rounded the corner to the women's accessories, she picked up a cashmere scarf and gently rubbed the soft fabric. "Looking for something special?" the woman asked, no longer pretending to be occupied with rearranging the items on a neighboring rack.

Again, Tessa brushed her off, saying that she just needed to pick out a few things, and hoping she'd finally get the point. Spotting other shoppers—what looked like a mother and daughter—a few aisles over, she mumbled about having a good holiday, and with a weak smile, was off to help the other customers.

Tessa watched as the younger of the two women explained that they were looking for something special for her grandmother. Her heart sunk, and she suddenly felt foolish holding the scarf just a few feet away. Her mind searched for the last gift she'd sent Nana, but she couldn't recall. She knew it was most likely something as superficial as the scarf in her hands. She'd had to wave the saleswoman off because she didn't have an answer to her question, "looking for something special?" Tessa didn't know what special was anymore.

She took the scarf from the display and grabbed a few other items from the store before heading to the busy checkout, swiping her credit card and ignoring the offers to spend more, save more that the saleswomen proposed. Back on the sidewalk, her red bag in hand, she started toward her apartment, feeling oddly defeated from shopping. She always bought lovely gifts with high price tags, but were they ever special?

When she reached a Jay's Jewelers, she placed two hands against the glass and peered into the display in the front window. Like the others, the brilliant pieces of jewelry shined throughout, but around them was so much more. There were images of people receiving gifts, their faces bright with a natural glow as they unwrapped their boxes. She pushed open the doors and walked throughout the store, trying to go unnoticed as she listened to shoppers share what they were looking for. One by one, each request was more personal than the last, with a woman near her saying that she needed something extra special for her mother—that it had been a hard year, and she wanted something that would make her smile.

Tessa stopped, listening to the woman's story, and watched as she pulled out something from her pocket and said, "can you do something with this?" Tessa strained her eyes and saw she was holding a wedding ring. As she looked over, the woman's head snapped in her direction, sending her swiftly in the opposite direction toward the exit.

Pushing through the doors without looking back, she was again on the streets, accompanied by the feeling that Jay may have been right—she had lost the meaning of Christmas. The decorations and lights surrounded her, the holiday suddenly hard to ignore. Feeling overwhelmed, she headed in the direction of her apartment, realizing that maybe it really was time to go back to Chestnut Ridge after all.

Chapter 3

Tessa sold her first car when she decided to move to New York and needed to finance the hefty security deposit on her first apartment. She considered it a step up at the time, thinking that a beat-up car for an apartment was more than an even trade. There was no reason to have a car in the city—it was a bigger burden thinking about where to park than it was to take a taxi. Though her mom was never able to wrap her head around that concept, finding it incomprehensible that someone could get around without a car. It was one of the many things she didn't quite understand about city life.

When Tessa told her she was going to schedule a ride back to Chestnut Ridge with a popular rideshare app at the cost of two hundred dollars, she nearly blew her gasket—partly from the price but mostly from the concept itself.

"You are going to let a *stranger* drive you all the way out here in their car? How could you possibly think that's a good idea? Is this how you're living up there in the city? All loosey-goosey? You're going to have me worried sick with this lifestyle."

Feeling a little more laid back than usual, and since she was home packing in sweatpants with a literal ban from thinking anything about work, she laughed. "How is it any different than if I schedule a ride with a car company? Those are strangers also."

"It's completely different! Those drivers are vetted. I don't know exactly what they do, but they at least get background checks, have company cars. These people on the app, what do they do? Just roll up in their Honda Civic ready to give you a ride?"

Occasionally her mom's small town views could be quite amusing. "Mom, they do background checks on the app also. It's a major company—they aren't going to let anything happen to one of their users. That would be, like, a major publicity issue. Plus, it uses your location services on your phone, so technically, even if I did get a ride from a crazy person, they would be able to track me down and find me based on the data on my phone."

"I don't care. No daughter of mine is driving all the way out to Chestnut Ridge with a stranger. I'll schedule a car service."

Tessa's mom hated driving in the city and anywhere else she considered dangerous, which was pretty much anywhere outside of Chestnut Ridge. The farthest she drove was on the one-lane, country route to the shopping mall over forty minutes away from her home.

Playing with her, Tessa said, "You know, Mom, you could come pick me up in the city." She knew she never would.

"Don't be ridiculous! I have way too much to do getting ready for your arrival. I've been searching the attic for hours for your special Christmas morning plate. Do you think I have time to drive all the way to get you? I'll schedule a car with someone down at Mr. Flatt's. Just be ready by 10:00 a.m. please—I don't need the driver searching for you all over the city."

Her mom had more traditions than she could count, and having a special plate for Christmas morning was just one of the ones for the holiday. "I don't need to have my special plate, I'm thirty years old. But I get your point, you're busy." After one more attempt, she resigned, saying, "If you insist, I'll be ready tomorrow by ten."

"Good! And don't you say such horrible things, It wouldn't be Christmas morning without our special plates. I can't wait to see you, sweetie, but gotta run! Tomorrow, 10:00 a.m."

And before Tessa could say goodbye, her mother was off the phone, presumably flitting back up to the attic in search of her childhood plate painted with a colorful gingerbread house. Each year when she was younger, her mom would pretend she couldn't remember which plate was Tessa's. She'd lay out the gingerbread plate at her or her nana's seat and put one of the others out in front of Tessa. When she was very young, she'd cry and insist that the snowman or reindeer wasn't hers. She'd try to convince them both by telling stories of previous years as they'd play along with each other, questioning whose was whose. As she got older, it became much more of a game amongst the three

50

of the them, and she herself would mix up the plates just for fun. It was just one of the many traditions her family had for the holidays. Christmas at the Gee home was a day filled with one tradition after the next, which was what made holidays such a special occasion and something to look forward to.

***

The next day at 10:00 a.m. sharp, she was standing in her lobby with an oversized suitcase and a large travel bag, scanning the street for anything that resembled a car that would be used with a car service.

Ride's out front, black car was the only information she received from her mom regarding her scheduled pick-up. She allowed the doorman to swing open the door to her building, pulling her suitcase out to the sidewalk behind her, when she stopped abruptly, the bag hitting her heel.

"Look who it is, Miss Tessa Gee." Zak Lawson, a classmate from Chestnut Ridge High School and best friend of Chase stood before her in a black jacket and driver's hat.

"*You* are my ride?" She asked, hoping even her mother would not be this obtuse to arrange her ex-boyfriend's best friend to drive her the two hours home.

"Yep, I work for the car company. You know the one by the mountain? When the call came in and I saw the name, I couldn't resist snagging up the ride and getting to drive Ms. Gee." He walked over to her luggage and briskly took it away and began loading it into the trunk. She stood back on the sidewalk, stiff with shock. Here she was ten years later standing before someone she once would have considered a great friend, not knowing what to say next. This trip back home was off to an awkward start. "You gonna get in the car or what? I mean, I can pick you up off the curb and put you in the car too if ya want?" Zak said jokingly as he opened the rear driver side door. Without saying anything, she walked over to the car and slipped into the backseat as Zak shut the door behind her and climbed in up front.

Looking from mirror to mirror for an opening to pull out into the traffic, he said, "I hate the city this time of year—actually any time of year. Too many cars and way too many people. I don't know how anyone lives here. It would drive me nuts."

She replied with a simple *mm-hmm* before digging into her purse for her cell phone. This was not the way she wanted to start out her trek back down memory lane to Chestnut Ridge. Five seconds in and she was already overwhelmed with déjà vu.

"I'm sorry. Guess I shouldn't be dissing your hometown," he teased.

"It's okay. I don't love all the people either. But it beats the pants off of Chestnut Ridge. There's more deer there than people. Who would want that?"

"Hey! I happen to like deer," he said, looking up into the rearview mirror with a smile.

"Then I guess it's the perfect place for you, Zak." She returned the same snide look.

He moved his attention to the road. "I guess it is then, isn't it. Want me to put on some music?"

"Whatever you feel like listening to is fine with me." He turned the knob, increasing the volume to a soft hum.

Zak Lawson, you kidding me, Mom?! She typed with both hands. *Not the way I wanted to start my trip!*

"Your mom wouldn't know the driver they were going to send . . ." He looked back up and winked at her in the rearview mirror. "When you call to book, they don't tell you."

Grunting, Tessa asked, "You spying on me or something?"

Zak shook his head. "I wouldn't dare. But it's not exactly like you tried to hide how unhappy you were to see me and I know your mom booked the ride, so I can assume."

Looking out the window, the city moving behind her as they drove toward the tunnel, she exhaled. "It's not that I'm unhappy to see you. I just haven't been home in a while."

Zak nodded as they headed into the tunnel, not pushing the issue any further for now.

She looked back down at her phone and scrolled through a few news headlines before the service froze midway across the river, leaving her screen stuck on an advertisement.

"You get service in here?" Zak asked in an obvious attempt at conversation.

"Not at the moment, no." She let her phone drop to her lap.

"So you're just looking down at that thing waiting for it to pop back to life?"

He was beginning to try her patience. "No, I have an article up that I can still see, if you must know."

Zak laughed and shook his head again.

"What now?" She asked, irritated.

"Nothing . . . Just thought you'd have a little more to say after over ten years."

Tessa rolled her eyes. "What would you like me to say? How've you been, where're you working? Ah! You bought a house—that's great! Then maybe I could lie and say that I'm so happy that you're thriving at the car company and living in a bi-level on the lake when really, we haven't spoken in over a decade, and if we're being honest, neither of us could care less about each other's drastically different lives. Does that cover it for you?"

Zak reached for the volume on the radio and turned up the cheery, holiday jingle playing over the speakers. "Well, since we got all that covered, guess it's Christmas music the rest of the way out."

"Perfect," Tessa said, slumping back in her seat with her arms crossed.

The car looped its way from the tunnel, past the skyline and started down the congested highway toward the tip of New Jersey. They'd have to follow all major roads until they ended and then continue on before they got anywhere near Chestnut Ridge. That was her least favorite part about the isolation of where she grew up—there was only one way in and one way out.

Her phone, back in service, buzzed on her lap. *How lovely!* ☺ *They didn't tell me that when I booked the car. Must be nice to see an old friend. Safe ride!* ☺

Misused emojis again followed up her mom's overjoyed message. Obviously, she totally missed Tessa's tone, or she was choosing to ignore it.

Feeling the guilt settle in, Tessa decided to let the car mishap go. She didn't want to be angry with her mom before she even got to the house. It was just going to be the two of them for almost two full weeks, and they hadn't spent that much time together since Tessa was in high school. She didn't need it getting off to a rocky start.

Surrendering, she typed, *We just got out of the city. See you soon.*

Zak tapped his fingers on the steering wheel as "Rockin' Around the Christmas Tree" hummed in the background. It was clear he had more he wanted to ask her, and it only took to the second verse before he started talking again.

"You think about home often?" he asked.

Considering his question, she said, "I mean, I think about my mom, yes. But not much else about Chestnut Ridge."

"You don't think about when you lived here? Memories, I guess. You think about anything like that?" He quickly glanced into the mirror before looking back down at the road.

"Are you asking if I think about high school? No. Why would I? Doesn't everyone hate high school?"

Zak snickered. "I didn't think it was that bad for you, Tess. There were a lot of good times."

58

She sat silent for a moment, thinking back to what she could remember. She had pushed so many memories of that time from her mind that she had to try hard to remember them. Zak was right—it wasn't all bad. She could remember a lot of happy memories mixed in with some sad. Both in her home life and out in her teenage years. She loved the time she'd spent with her nana and Mom—the ease of Sunday dinners that filled her up with her Italian favorites and sitting out on her back deck in the summer, listening to the music coming from the woods behind her house. There were kisses by the lake, and plenty of nights laid out on blankets, looking up at the stars with Chase. Zak was right, there were plenty of good times. But she was always so focused on getting out of Chestnut Ridge, focused on doing something bigger and better, so those memories had to be pushed aside. They were tucked away someplace in the back of her mind, where she only thought of them if prompted. When she left that August, Chase standing in her driveway, waving with that sad smile, she knew it would be hard to return. And from the way he watched her pull away, she knew Chase felt it too, that it was over between them.

"He's doing pretty good, ya know," Zak interrupted.

"Who?" she asked, blinking quickly, returning back to her current situation.

"Chase . . . He's doing pretty darn good. Got his own business and everything. I work with him too, or . . . did you think I was really just a driver for a car company?"

Feeling more aware of her quickness to judge, she said, "I guess I didn't ask, did I?"

"No, you assumed. Which is fair, I suppose, given our current set up."

This time she laughed. "You can't blame me too much, can you? You are my driver home."

"Guess not. *Well, what do you do, Zak?*" he mocked. "Thanks for asking, Tess. I am an electrician, and Chase owns a contracting business. He's done very well building out the neighborhoods a little bit outside of Chestnut Ridge. You know

60

the ones that the hipsters are buying into to get away from the smog? All you city folks are moving back out to the country and want custom homes, and that has been great for business." He laughed. "Chase's company builds the homes, contracts me, and I light them up. I drive to help out Mr. Flatts—he's my neighbor now and is getting pretty old, and he asked if I'd do a few rides on the weekends. You remember Mr. Flatts, don't you? From the big old house that gave out king-size candy for Halloween?"

She did remember Mr. Flatts and his huge house on the hill that all the children would flock to with their pillowcases. He was always generous within the community and was involved in many of the special activities for kids growing up in Chestnut Ridge, including the town's Christmas tree lighting and the children's pageant that was put on each year. He lived in one of the best neighborhoods in the town, and if Zak was his neighbor, then he must be doing darn good as an electrician. And if Chase hires him, that means he must be doing even better.

"Well, Zak, I am happy for you then. Sounds like you are doing really great."

"Now, you're not going to expect me to believe that after that outburst, are ya?"

"I mean it!" she said, slapping the back of the driver seat. "I apologized and, not for nothing, you haven't exactly asked much about my life either!"

"Point taken. How are you, Tess? How's life in the big city?" he quipped.

"It's wonderful. I work for a large firm, have an office and an assistant, work on the best accounts . . . the whole nine."

Zak nodded, pretending he was interested. "And your personal life? Married? Kids?"

"Goodness no, I don't really have time for too much outside of work. Plus no one gets married this early in New York. But I do have my own apartment in a great neighborhood, so that's something, right?"

"I guess so. Seems kinda boring to me, but to each their own," he trailed. "I'm happy for you then . . . you and your apartment in a good neighborhood." It didn't sound bad, but it also didn't sound like a compliment.

"What about you—do you have a family?" she asked, already knowing the answer. Based on his social media profile, he was married to a girl who was a grade behind them in school and they had two kids, which he confirmed.

The two made small talk for the rest of the way to Chestnut Ridge, reminiscing on old memories and past times, including many nights their group of friends had spent together on the lake.

When they reached the end of the main road, Zac turned down the heavily-wooded single lane that lead to Chestnut Ridge. The road wound through the mountains, zigzagging its way past the tall trees that lined each side. At the very end, right before you reached the town, the trees cleared at the top of a steep hill with Chestnut Ridge sitting directly below, tucked in the valley of the mountains. Tessa looked up out the front window, eyes wide, forgetting just how quaint the town was. From up here, it looked like it could be featured on the front of a Christmas card, offering cozy sentiments of the season.

A blanket of snow covered the town from the end of October straight through to April. It may not snow every day, but it never melted from the ground. Once the first storm dropped in during the fall, you wouldn't see the grass again until the spring. Though there wasn't much to the town, it did have a cozy feel. From up top on the hill, you could see the smoke swirling from the chimneys—many houses came with either a fireplace or wood burning stove. Most of the town was concealed by tall pines with a few clearings near the lakes, which were frozen over for the winter.

As they drove through the town, Zak pointed out things that were the same from when they were growing up and listed off what had changed, noting just a few additions to the small town square.

By the time she pulled up to her mom's house on Lakeview Road, they seemed like old friends again. After pulling up the long driveway, he stopped the car, jumped out, and fetched her suitcases from the truck before opening her door. She stepped out, her heel slipping slightly on the iced-over driveway, and she grabbed the door to steady herself.

"Forgot about how cold it gets up here, huh?" Zak said. "Could barely be snowing in the city, but out here we'll have a foot."

"I guess I did forget," she said as she reached into her purse for her wallet.

"Don't you even think about tipping me, Tess. It was good to catch up, that's enough for me."

"Don't be silly! Mr. Flatts paying you that well?"

"Well enough that I don't need your money," he said smiling. "Welcome back to Chestnut Ridge."

"Not back," she corrected. "Just visiting." She grabbed the handle of her suitcase. "I'll give you a five-star review, how's that?"

"Works for me," he said. "And make sure to tell your mom hi." He opened the driver door and sat back in the driver seat. She started toward the walkway to the front door, but he called after her. "Hey, Tess, think about calling Chase, would ya? It's just him since his mom passed, and I think he'd love to hear from you."

She nodded, not wanting to commit to a definitive yes or no answer and turned back toward the front walkway to the house.

"I mean it!" he yelled, as he slammed the door.

This time she didn't turn back but continued up to the front steps. Her mom had come out on the porch and was now waving like crazy at Zak as he slowly backed out of the driveway. She stopped and smiled down at her and said, "Welcome home, my love!"

Smiling, Tessa let out a deep sigh. "Thanks, Mom, it's good to be here."

"It's even better to have you! This is going to be the most magical two weeks! Hope you're ready for it, Tessy. We're going to have so much fun!"

"Oh, Mom! You know I hate when you call me Tessy!" she whined, cringing from the nickname.

She pulled her in for a hug and held her tight. "Dear, I do know, and you should know I couldn't care less!" She laughed as she shuffled her in the front door. When she entered the main foyer area, everything looked like the last time she was home. The walls were filled with pictures of her from her childhood, and a few candles comfortingly burned letting off faint smells of Christmas, only to be overpowered by the scent of her mom's cooking drafting its way down the hall from the kitchen. For the first time in a long time she felt herself relax, if only slightly.

"Smells delicious, Mom!" she said, walking back toward the kitchen. She may be nervous to be back in Chestnut Ridge, but it sure was good to be home.

Chapter 4

"Do you mind giving the tomato sauce a stir?" her mom asked, as she pulled a tray of chicken parmesan from the oven. "I don't want the bottom to burn. Nana would come back just to whack me with the spoon for letting that happen to her sauce recipe!"

With a glass of wine in one hand, Tessa grabbed the wooden spoon and slowly stirred the sauce in the oversized pot her mom had bubbling on the stove.

"Are you cooking for the entire neighborhood or just me and you?" she joked.

"You know I like to make plenty of sauce," her mom piped back as she playfully hit her with the dish towel. "Have you forgotten what it's like to sit down and have a good meal? You're wasting away. Look at you, you're skin and bones!"

Tessa hadn't noticed in New York, but here in her mom's kitchen she did see that her frame was thinning, her collar bones more noticeable than they had been before. "I tell you all the time that I'm busy, and I definitely don't have time to cook. I usually just eat a salad or something for dinner."

"A girl can't live on lettuce alone, but don't you worry, we're going to be cooking up a storm here the next few days so we'll plump you right back up!" her mother said with excitement as she tossed an al dente rigatoni pasta in extra virgin olive oil.

After helping set the table, she poured another glass of pinot noir for each of them, then sat in her usual seat with her mom at the head. Maybe it was the smell of garlic or the delicious meal in front of her, but she could practically see her nana sitting across the table as she used to. Growing up they had quite the routine, the three of them. Every night they'd sit down over one of Nana's meticulously-created meals and talk about their days. While most of her friends' diets were chock full of chicken nuggets and hot dogs, Tessa ate like a queen six days a week—but Fridays, just for her, they ordered pizza. Her nana always said that dinner was the most important time of the day. With her busy schedule of school activities and play dates, it was the one time the three of them always spent together. Though her mom was always present, her nana was the one that would make sure she finished her plate, including the vegetables she hated. Nana was too hard to deny. In their home, it was her way or no way, and no one ever went against it out of love for her. Nana also had a knack for reminding you of those less fortunate, and Tessa felt bad complaining about broccoli after a story her nana would tell of children who went hungry.

"This looks delicious," she said as she helped herself to two pieces of chicken and a generous portion of pasta. She didn't want to admit it, but she really was tired of the mundane salads she prepared for herself. If it wasn't for client meals, her palette would be completely out of practice. It took little to convince her that she was overdue for some carbs and cheese.

"Tessy, guess what. I pulled out Nana's book and went through all the recipes we'll need. We can do some baking tomorrow so we'll have cookies to give out around the neighborhood and at the pageant. Then we'll have to cook a few trays for the tree lighting and, of course, our delicious seafood feast for Christmas Eve! I can't even begin to tell you how excited I am to cook up these recipes with you. Since you haven't been coming home, I've been keeping it quite simple around the holidays, but my stomach is growling for some old-fashioned, Gee holiday food."

"That sounds great, Mom. I can't believe you have her recipe book. I haven't seen it in years. Remember when Nana and I tried to make every recipe that one summer? I think we got just a few pages in and I got bored and moved on to a new project."

Her mother laughed at the memory. "Don't blame yourself. She probably scared you away. She ran a tight kitchen."

"Oh, she did," Tessa said, taking a sip of wine. "Remember that one year we made hundreds of cookies? We were so excited to start, but by the afternoon I was covered in flour and exhausted and there she was, still rolling out her dough to perfection."

"That year was insane! I think we had cookies for the entire town."

"Well, I think that's how she would have liked it—the entire town eating her cookies."

They both fell silent and returned to their plates, Tessa scraping up every last bit of spaghetti sauce before saying, "It certainly hasn't been the same without her, has it?"

"No. It hasn't," her mom agreed.

After the dishes were done and they'd watched one episode of a crime show on television, Tessa was upstairs in her childhood room, tucked away in her childhood bed. Her Christmas nightlight, an angel that looked like it could top a tree, spread a warm light over the room. Swapping out the nightlight was another childhood tradition. One year, after having a horrible nightmare, she ran down the hall and begged her nana to let her sleep with her. Instead she pulled the angel light from her own wall and plugged it in in Tessa's room, promising that no angel would ever allow a nightmare to break through to a child's dreams near Christmas. From that night on, she slept soundly under the watchful glow.

Looking around her room, it was like it was stuck in time—it was almost exactly how it looked before leaving for college. Her walls were still plastered with pictures of her high school friends, and of course, there were plenty of pictures of Chase. If she didn't know it was over ten years later, it would feel like she was back in her room those last nights that August, packing up her clothes as she snuck text messages out to him, since she wasn't allowed to be on the phone after 11:00 p.m.

Even then, Tessa had little confidence that she and Chase could make their relationship work throughout college and afterward. She loved him—still got butterflies just thinking about him—but she knew they wanted different things, and there was no number of butterflies that could overcome that. Simply put, she wanted something more out of life. Chase didn't share in her need to flee their hometown and was the epitome of a small-town boy.

He played football during the fall and baseball in the spring and was captain of both teams as a senior. Throughout high school they'd spent hours wrapped up in each other's arms talking about what they wanted for their future, and the older they got the clearer it became to her that they weren't on the same page. If she'd stayed close to Chestnut Ridge, they'd have gotten married, built a house in a new neighborhood, and had kids of their own by now. While it was the American dream for most, it wasn't hers.

Chase left for college a few days after she did, and in the first few weeks, things seemed promising, like what they had could maybe last. They'd called each other daily, speaking of how they were adjusting to college life and making new friends, careful not to make the other jealous. But the time in between the calls grew, and within the first month, late after a freshman mixer, she e-mailed him saying that she wanted to end things and go their separate ways. When she received his reply—a simple OK—she assumed he had felt it too, or that he had found someone else. So she spent the next ten years trying to replace him, and she never could.

Tessa rolled to the side of her bed and reached under it, searching for a box she had pushed far to the back the last time she was home. Her hands fumbled around, eventually finding the box and pulling it out, placing it on the edge of her bed. Lifting the cover, she pushed through the few items she'd stored that reminded her of their relationship and found the photo she was looking for. It was after the prom, and her hair was still knotted on top of her head in a mess of curls, though they were both in sweatshirts in the photo. She was sitting, her legs pretzeled, and Chase had an arm around her, his other on her knee, and was kissing her cheek. They were in their favorite spot, a remote area near the lake where they liked to spend their time. Tucked away from the beaches and bike trails, there was nothing in this area but a single park bench and an open plot of sandy grass that led down to the lake's jagged edge. Not only was it their favorite place, it was her favorite picture of them together, and possibly the last. Looking at her face, she knew she was happy. Jess, one of her best friends, and some of their other friends were there that night, but she recalled feeling like it was just Chase and her, sitting under the stars after a magical night of swaying to the music at the prom. It was the kind of spring night where it felt like summer, the temperature perfect if you had a sweatshirt. With her hand in his, she remembered not wanting the night to end, knowing that things were never going to be that simple again.

After putting the picture back in the box, she closed it tight, then tucked it back under her bed. She tried to push it as far toward the back as she could, where she wouldn't be able to reach it for the rest of her trip home.

Chapter 5

"Tessa! You up?" her mom yelled from the bottom of the stairs. "I have coffee and breakfast coming out soon!"

She rolled over and rubbed her eyes before looking at her phone—it was after eight and she couldn't remember the last time she'd slept in this late. Swinging her legs from the bed, she opened the door a crack and yelled that she'd be down soon, then headed back into her room to clean up a bit before she going downstairs.

In her bathroom—having her own was a perk of being an only child—she splashed water on her face and brushed her teeth quickly, glancing up at her reflection in the mirror. The skin on her face seemed thin and stretched, dark circles hanging from under her eyes. She noticed a few creases on her forehead that seemed to have deepened—that in the rush of her normal morning routine she had missed. Stepping away from the mirror an inch or so, she looked back at herself and observed how she had aged since most of the photos in her room. Ten years, a stressful job, long nights with little sleep, and city smog could definitely do a number on your skin. She brushed through her hair before knotting it on the top of her head, put on her bathrobe, securing it tight at her waist, and walked downstairs.

"Morning, Tessy," her mom said as she whisked a sauce on top of the stove. "I'm making another one of your favorites—homemade biscuits with sausage gravy."

Tessa grabbed a mug from the cabinet and filled it from the pot of fresh coffee. "I don't think I've had anything that rich since I left Chestnut Ridge. There's a chance my stomach will flat-out reject it."

"Oh, please! Don't be silly. Calories don't count around Christmas."

Tessa broke into laughter at the thought. "If only that was true. It would be what I asked for every year." She walked over to the stove and looked down at the pot, steaming with the breakfast her nana would say made her stomach sing. The gravy and biscuits smelled delightful, and her stomach may not be singing, but it was certainly yearning for a full plate of what she was smelling.

Her mom took out a pan of golden-brown biscuits and placed them on top of the stove.

"Perfect!" she exclaimed, clearly pleased with the coloring.

Tessa pulled at the corner of one of the biscuits, snagging a buttery, flaky piece that she popped in her mouth as her mother smacked at her hand.

"I give 'em a nine," she said as she chewed.

"Only a nine? Tough critic."

Her mother reached for the two plates she had laid out on the counter and split a biscuit in half on each before smothering both sides in the thick, decadent gravy, sprinkled with bits of maple sausage.

"Try a little of this, then see what score you'd give me," she said, handing her the plate and a fork.

Tessa sliced into the biscuit and dragged it along the gravy, soaking up a fair amount before putting it in her mouth.

"Wow! I forgot how good this was!" She quickly sliced a second piece, topping it with even more gravy.

"Well don't eat the whole plate standing here by the stove. Go sit, enjoy it." Her mom swatted her away and toward the table.

Tessa grabbed the ladle in the sauce pot and poured a heaping amount of gravy over what was left on her plate. Her mom smiled and shook her head before waving her off to sit.

Moments later, as she stuffed her face with the sweet sausage gravy, her mom came back into the kitchen holding her nana's cookbook. The oversized book looked exactly as she remembered it. The bright red cover that read *Recipes* across the top, hand stitched by her nana. The rigid pages, uneven as they stuck out the side, were the additional recipes Nana had shoved in over the years, copied down from friends, family, and other cooks she'd considered trusted sources.

Her mom placed it down on the table in front of her, and they both stared down at it for a moment before Tessa reached for its edge and slid it back across the table to her. To anyone else the recipe book wouldn't appear to be much, but that was not the case for her. It was such a staple in her life and was considered her nana's most prized possession. She'd always spoken of how she'd spent a lifetime collecting and perfecting the recipes that it held, and that its contents were top secret and only few could be trusted to look inside. The only people Tessa ever saw Nana open the book in front of was her and her mom. Occasionally, a church friend would ask to look at one of her recipes, and Nana would come home in a huff at the audacity of the request. For the next few days, she'd carry her recipe book with her around the house, as if she could let it out of sight and her friend would snatch it up to read its contents.

"Nana loved her recipes, didn't she? I feel like this was her bible," she said running her hand along the edges. "I always remember it out, propped up on the counter, flipped open to whatever recipe she planned to cook."

Her mom nodded and sipped her coffee as Tessa flipped through the pages in the book, looking closely at each as she passed. She could practically taste and smell the recipes as she read the names off the pages. From homemade sauces, to roasts, to pastas and desserts, each recipe was more scrumptious than the next. Growing up, she had loved every one of them. There wasn't a single dish she could think of that she wouldn't devour if Nana made it.

"I don't even know where I'd start, trying to learn to cook like her," Tessa said. "I can't make anything even close to one of the recipes in this book."

"You loved cooking and baking with her, Tessy. You guys were always together concocting something at the stove! Half the time I felt left out, like the kitchen was a club for just the two of you." Her mom paused and touched her hand on the edge of the recipe book. "I'm sure it would all come back if you tried making something other than a salad. I don't know what that city has done to you that you eat like a little rabbit. You were raised to believe food is love."

"Sadly, my waistline doesn't love food," she said, poking her side. "But maybe that's true . . . If I tried again, it would come back." Tessa turned the page to one of her favorite seafood dishes Nana used to make on Christmas Eve. "What are we going to start with? You said we were going to do it all, so where do we start?"

Her mom stood and turned the book toward her, and she flipped back through a few pages before tapping the page labeled *Cookies*. "We're going to need some treats to hand out around town, so I think we start with cookies."

Tessa chuckled sarcastically. "You know baking was always my least favorite. I hate how you have to be so precise. Who wants to measure a fourth of a teaspoon of something? But if that's where you want to start, that's where we'll start." She considered herself unskilled when it came to cooking, but baking was even worse. Even when Tessa had tried to bake with Nana, she'd have to follow behind her, correcting the mismarked ingredients or heaping spoonfuls that should have been neat.

"Perfect!" her mom said as she began pulling items from the fridge. "Do you mind running out for some more butter? I didn't realize how much went into that darn gravy this morning, and we're going to need more for the cookies."

"I would, but are you forgetting that I don't have my car?"

"Take mine!" she answered, without looking up. "You know I hate going to the market on the weekends. It gets so crowded. Way too many people."

Tessa pictured the store in the city, the aisles bursting with crazed customers trying to get the last organic, non-GMO almond butter. The local market would be nothing compared to that.

"Sure, I'll shower up then head out."

Her mom turned to look at her, a bright smile crossing her face. "I'm so excited to do this with you, Tessy. I just want you to know that it means so much to me."

Tessa returned the smile and nodded before heading up the stairs to her bathroom. She tried to remember the last time she'd had something for breakfast other than black coffee and an occasional banana. It was barely 10 in the morning and she was already stuffed full. She was going to be two sizes bigger if she kept this up for the next two weeks.

When she got to her room she peaked at her cell phone and saw that she had a notification from Ben. A familiar twinge of anxiety about missing a message from her boss returned as she quickly accessed her e-mail.

Meeting with Jay's Jewelers scheduled for next week to discuss the upcoming year. Just keeping you in the loop. Deal still stands, no e-mails. Just thought you should know where we're at with the client.

From habit, she began typing out a response and stopped midway to consider whether to send—Ben did say no e-mail. Ultimately, not answering her boss didn't sit well with her so she finished her response.

We already had their year-end wrap up. Everything alright? Do you need me back in the city?

Ben was quick to respond.

You're on paid time off. No e-mail. You need this, Tess.

Tessa didn't understand Ben's logic. He was the one who e-mailed her, dropping that her biggest client requested a last-minute meeting to discuss the future. How could she not respond?

Frustrated, she was going to remind Ben that he started the chain, but instead she threw her phone onto her bed and pulled her shirt over her head to jump in the shower. This time away from work was going to be hard regardless, but now she had this meeting lingering in her mind and she was bound to overanalyze what it meant. Ben did smooth it over with Jay for now, but that didn't mean they'd stay on with the firm long-term. The last thing she needed was to lose such a big client over her lack of holiday cheer.

After getting dressed in leggings and an oversized sweater, Tessa grabbed the keys from her mom and headed out to the garage. She hadn't driven a car in years and hoped it was like riding a bike or any other skill you never really lost.

She turned on the ignition, switched the car into reverse, and slowly pulled out of the garage and driveway. By the time she was on the main road from her house, she was more comfortable and was cruising at a solid thirty miles per hour, a safe speed for the icy roads.

When she got to the market, she found a spot close to the walkway and pulled in and put the car in park, though she found herself unable to turn off the car and make her way inside. Chestnut Ridge was even smaller than the average small town, and she suddenly realized she had a high probability of running into someone she'd once known in the store. Her distaste for the town was not the common opinion, and most of her classmates and friends had stayed back in Chestnut Ridge. Her mom and Nana would update her from time to time on the happenings of the people she used to be close with, commenting on how they understood why they stayed—it was a beautiful place to build a life and raise a family. At home in her apartment, she'd roll her eyes and laugh at the thought of those who chose not to leave, but being back, she felt like an outsider.

Tessa reached up and pulled down the visor to check herself in the mirror, instantly regretting not taking the time to put on mascara and maybe a little blush. She took a deep breath and forced herself out of the car, hoping not to bump into anyone she knew.

With her head down, she walked through the automatic doors and headed straight for the butter, grabbing two large containers because she couldn't remember how much her mom had asked for.

She walked up an empty aisle and approached the cashier. She might actually make it out of the store without seeing anyone she knew. After grabbing her receipt and bag, she wrapped her scarf around her neck and headed out to the car.

Back in the lot, she briskly walked over to her mom's car and plopped down in the driver's seat. Without looking, Tessa backed up the car only to be startled by a loud honk and thud that followed.

Frozen, she turned to look and saw Mr. Weaver waving an angry fist out his window. He had been known as the town's old grump back when she was in school—God knows what another decade has done for his far-from-pleasant personality. Gearing the car from reverse to drive, she pulled back into the parking spot, turned the car off, and got out to assess the damage.

"I'm so sorry, Mr. Weaver. I didn't see you there." Tessa said, hoping to quickly dissolve the scene he was creating.

"What are you, blind? I was right here, just driving along and WHAM! You back up right into my car," he yelled.

"I know, and I'm so sorry. I haven't driven in a while and am still getting used to it," she said, pulling her scarf tighter around her neck.

"That's not an excuse. Look at my car!"

Tessa looked down at the side bumper that she had tapped and searched for any sign of the incident. "To be honest, I don't see any damage."

"Oh, you don't?" Mr. Weaver's voice elevated, and he was now rambling about her stupidity.

"I said I'm sorry. Let me see if my mom has her insurance card in the glove compartment."

"Just perfect!" he called after her. "You're not even going to pay for this!"

Flustered, Tessa, scrambled through her purse looking for her phone to call her mom as Mr. Weaver continued to kick at the snow beside her. She tried to tell him she would be happy to sort it out, she just had to get her mom on the phone, but he was relentless. She could feel her face turning Christmas red as she listened to the phone ring and ring, her mom clearly too busy in the kitchen to pick up.

"I . . . I, I just have to . . ." Tessa felt like she could cry— here she was hoping to slip in and out of the store, and now she was part of a huge scene attracting attention in the parking lot.

"Mr. Weaver!" she heard a familiar voice say. "What's the problem here?"

Mr. Weaver turned and looked back. Chase was approaching them from the far side of the lot. "The problem is that this lady just hit my car, and she isn't going to pay for it. And now I'm late getting home for my shows."

Chase looked over at Tessa and smiled his perfect smile. "Is that so?"

Tessa's heart skipped a beat at the playful tone in his voice. "Of course I would pay! I'm just trying to reach my mom. I'm not sure where she has the insurance information. The car's not mine. But I also don't see any damage . . . That's all I was trying to say."

Chase nodded with a wink before bending down to look at the bumper. He rubbed his hand along the metal and got in close, clearly putting on a show for Mr. Weaver. "I gotta agree with Tess here, sir. Doesn't look like there's any damage to the car."

Mr. Weaver bent over slightly and squinted to look closely. "I guess you're right . . . But I still missed the start of my shows because of this mess."

Chase stood and brushed a bit of snow from his knee. "I'm sure Miss Gee is very sorry about that, right, Tess?"

Tessa nodded her head. "Of course I am. I'm sorry I held you up, Mr. Weaver, and I'm sorry for backing into you."

Mr. Weaver grunted and walked back around to the driver side of his car. He slumped down into the seat and drove off as Chase waved after him.

Tessa bit her bottom lip, not knowing what to say next. Often she'd imagined scenarios about the next time she saw Chase, but she never could have dreamed up this one.

Chase turned back toward her and smiled again, causing her stomach to flip.

"Thank you," she said, as he waved her off.

"It was my pleasure. Anything for you, Tess."

They looked at each other, clearly not knowing what to say next. Uncomfortable with the silence between them, she asked how he had been, though she already knew. She looked him up more than she cared to admit.

When he finished the rundown, he thanked her for asking and said, "What about you? What's big city Tessa Gee been up to these days? Other than upsetting the town grump?"

With a nervous laugh, she suddenly wished she had more going on in her life. Chase had a business, owned a home, had a dog. All she had to show for herself was a job she'd been pushed away from and a small, ridiculously-overpriced apartment that barely had decent water pressure.

"Not too much, actually. I'm working at the same firm," she said, unsure if he knew as much about her as she did him. It was possible he was completely over her and didn't know much about her at all. "You know, just living up in the city," she finished, stumbling slightly over her words.

"That's great, Tess. Zak said he drove you in yesterday. Small world, huh?" he said with his hands in his front pockets.

"I think it's more like small town."

"Come on," he said. "What do you mean by that?"

Tessa laughed. "Just that only in Chestnut Ridge would my mom accidently hire my ex-boyfriend's best friend to be my driver home."

Chase flinched slightly when she said ex, but nodded with a grin. "Well, based on what happened here, I'd say hiring a driver was probably for the best. But I get it, it's hard to *really* get away from here and everyone, I guess."

"Yes, it is." It seemed they both understood they were talking about so much more.

Chase booted at the slush in the parking lot, his eyes down. "Well it was good seeing you. You look great, Tess. I mean that." He stepped in and put a single hand on her hip and kissed her cheek. She had to stop her arms from wrapping around him and pulling him in closer. Though years had passed, his touch felt the same and sent a tingle up her neck. He was taller and had filled out a bit since he was eighteen, but he was still Chase. She might be reading into it, but for a second, she thought he didn't want to let go. But he did. As he turned to walk away she yelled after him.

"It was really good to see you too."

He turned, looked back over his shoulder, and said, "Well, hopefully it's not the last time. Like you said, it is Chestnut Ridge." He then turned and headed into the store, stopping to speak to a few other people in the front near the entrance.

Back in the car, she once again pulled down the visor mirror and pressed at the bags under her eyes. She didn't look horrible, but she didn't look great either. Though Chase did say so, but he was probably just being nice. She would have much preferred to see him in her own element, wearing a pencil skirt and heels, looking every part of the successful business woman that she was. But instead she was in an old, ratty sweater, hair pulled back, fighting with Mr. Weaver in the parking lot, an eternity from where she felt confident. Lately it seemed if she didn't have bad luck, she wouldn't have any type of luck at all. Either way, it was good to see him—he looked incredible. Better than any of her recent dates in the city, but she would keep that to herself for now.

Chapter 6

"Mom!" Tessa kicked off her boots at the door. "You're never going to believe who I bumped into at the store, and looking like this, no less, making matters so much worse." Tessa dropped the butter onto the counter, still in the bag, next to her mom.

"Well first off, you look great," she said, pulling at Tessa's sweater. "And based on how much you care, I'm going to guess that you bumped into Chase."

"Is it really that obvious?" Tessa huffed.

Her mom looked back at her with a telling smile before reaching into the bag and pulling out the sticks of butter to soften on the counter.

"I just was hoping that the first time we ran into each other, I'd look, you know, like awesome and successful . . . like I made it. But instead, when I see him I'm looking like a mess without makeup on, while Mr. Weaver is flipping out on me in the parking lot at the market."

Her mom couldn't hold back her laughter. "Time to get even messier. These cookies aren't going to bake themselves," she said, tossing an apron her way. "Why was Mr. Weaver yelling at you?"

Tessa tied the apron around her waist, forming a bow at the center in front, and rolled up her sleeves. "Oh yeah, I backed into his car in the parking lot. BUT"—she yelled, before her mom could overreact—"there was no damage and everything worked out fine. Mr. Weaver was being completely unreasonable and was upset he missed his shows or something. Luckily, Chase was there and calmed him down. It was so embarrassing."

"I think it sounds like a very cute meet up!" her mom exclaimed, clapping her hands. "Sounds so much better than if you had bumped into him all done up like you made it, or however you described it. Much more natural this way. And what does that even mean? Looking like you made it?"

Tessa paused, not exactly sure what she meant by it. "I just want him to know that I did it, that I got out of Chestnut Ridge and made something of myself and am happy . . . That's all."

"*Mm-hmm*, I see." Her mom mumbled something else as she began mixing the dough with a large spoon.

"I don't mean anything by it, Mom. It's just that I left and he stayed, and then the way we ended things. Or I should say the way I ended things . . ." Tessa slumped in a chair at the table and tucked the hair that fell in front of her eyes behind her ears. "I've always felt a little bad that I broke up with him when I was at college and that we never saw each other after. I'm assuming that was hard on him."

"I'm sure it was." Tessa's mom flipped through the pages in Nana's book, trying to find the recipe she wanted to start with and seeming anxious to change the topic so she didn't say too much.

Her mom never made an attempt to hide how she felt about Tessa's decision to leave Chase. Not that she thought they should've settled in and gotten married either. She was just quick to point out that after spending three years together in a relationship, he deserved better than to be dumped over e-mail. Tessa didn't disagree, but back then she felt she would never be able to go through with it if he was standing in front of her. She had tried to end things a few times over the summer, but each night as they cuddled up to watch a movie, or sipped on sodas over a burger, she couldn't bring herself to do it. She'd always felt too happy, too comfortable. Too in love with him to have the nerve to leave him.

If it wasn't for the courage from the wine coolers or the miles between them, her hiding behind her computer, they'd probably still be together.

"What should we start with? The peanut blossoms—those are your favorite, aren't they?" her mom asked, as she reached for the peanut butter, scooping it out into the dough she'd already started in a bowl.

"Sure, I do like those and they're easy enough." Tessa stood from her seat at the table, happy to change the conversation.

As her mom mixed the dough, Tessa read Nana's notes on the page. Her handwriting was always neat but had gotten shaky over the years. This being one of her newer recipes in the book, you could tell she was aging as she wrote out her swirling cursive notes. Tessa touched the picture of the cookies that was taped to the left page, the recipe and notes on the right. When she had gotten her first camera, Nana asked her to help fill up the book with pictures of her recipes. Tessa was overjoyed and would carefully search for the right angle and lighting as she photographed her nana's food. The pictures were far from perfect, but Nana had always loved them, swearing she could have a career as a food stylist. She'd flip through the snapshots and pick three or four favorites, ultimately letting Tessa choose the photo that got taped in the book.

"Do you want to start unwrapping the chocolate kisses to put on top?"

"Sure! It's probably best if I stay away from the oven for the baking." She took the bag from her mom and sat back at the table, unwrapping each chocolate kiss, one by one.

"I don't remember you being a bad baker," her mom said. "Then again, I do seem to remember things a bit differently than you, so that makes sense."

Tessa pulled the foil from the pieces of chocolate, tossing them into a clear bowl once she was done. "What's that supposed to mean?"

"Nothing sweetheart . . . just that I don't think things were as bad around here as you remember. We had a lovely little life— you, me, and Nana."

Tessa could feel her increasingly-sour mood begin to show on her face as she tried to concentrate on her task. She and her mom bickered often about Chestnut Ridge and the life she had here.

"I never said it was bad at all. I just don't like being here."

"Exactly. Don't you think that hurts for the rest of us you left behind? How you couldn't wait to run away and be rid of us? How we have to drag you back here, kicking and screaming, only for you to talk down about every little thing going on in this town. I can only speak for myself, but I can say that it doesn't feel all that great."

The frustration had burned through, her face now hot with anger. "You don't have to *drag* me back here. I'm just busy and can't pop over for dinner every other night of the week. I just don't like Chestnut Ridge. It has nothing to do with you . . . you don't have to take everything personally."

Her mom huffed and turned from the mixer. "I don't think I'm the only one who took it personally when you shut the door on Chestnut Ridge and everyone who lives here. I know Nana felt bad. Sure, she always said she was proud of her petunia, out there on her own in the big world, but I knew that she missed you. She hardly got to spend any time with you those last few years."

"I called Nana all the time," Tessa interrupted, not willing to give her mom that one.

"A phone call isn't the same as seeing someone in person. You know that. And what about Chase, that poor kid. Can you imagine being dumped through an e-mail? That was cold, Tessa, and who knows if he's recovered. I don't think he's dated someone since."

Tessa, ready to speak, was silenced by the thought of Chase not being with anyone else since her. She doubted it was true, yet her heart skipped a beat over the thought.

"I'm sure he's just fine. He's probably dated lots of women around here. And Nana was happy for me—I know she was." Tessa traced the photo in the recipe book. All her nana ever wanted was for her to follow her dreams, no matter where they led her.

"Of course she was, Tess. Doesn't mean that she didn't miss you while you were away."

Tessa could only nod to show she understood, not able to argue that wasn't true. She was sure Nana did miss her—she missed her nana every day. Nana always offered the best advice and had the perfect answer for any problem. Though she didn't believe it, she was the smartest woman Tessa knew, and though it may have been mostly over the phone, a day didn't go by that they didn't speak.

"And I'm right about Chase too. This is Chestnut Ridge, after all. I'd know if he had been out with other people, but that hasn't been the case." She turned and locked eyes with Tessa. "There's been no one serious since you."

Involuntarily, Tessa smiled, quickly closing her lips when she realized it. It's not that she wanted Chase to be alone or unhappy, but for years the thought of him getting over her so easily worried her mind.

"It doesn't matter if he's dating or not. It's not like we're going to get back together after all this time. We hardly know each other." Sadly, that was the truth. She didn't know who he was after over ten years. "We were pretty much kids when we were together, and we're all grown up now. I'm sure he's forgotten all about me and just hasn't found the right person."

"I don't feel like fighting, Tess. Sometimes it's just hard to listen to how much you hate it here. This is where I wanted to raise you, and I made that choice and don't regret it." She reached down for the recipe book and flipped to the first page of the cookie recipes. "But we don't need to get into all that today. It's only your first day here and I just wanted to make some cookies with you, my daughter, who I have missed very much. Can we just do that?"

Tessa reached across the table, grabbed another handful of chocolates, and smiled up at her mother. "Absolutely. Now, how many batches of the Peanut Blossom recipe do we usually make?"

After agreeing that the recipe usually made between two and three batches, they took out two large cookie sheets and began to spoon the dough onto the pans. Carefully, they lined up the tiny mounds of dough into even rows and sprinkled the tops with granulated sugar before placing them in the oven.

While the cookies baked in the oven, they chose an additional four recipes to bake that day, giving them five options total. Though it was hard to choose—the book easily had over twenty Christmas cookie recipes—they decided on chocolate chip, gingerbread, chocolate crinkle cookies, and biscotti. They selected those mostly because they were difficult to mess up and didn't require the skill or precision some of the others did.

By three o'clock, with three recipes down, they needed a break. Her mom poured out two large glasses of milk that they clinked together to cheers their success, while biting into a warm cookie.

"We're not doing so bad, are we?" her mom asked.

Tessa scanned the kitchen table at the plates piled high with cookies. "I'd say we're doing pretty darn good."

Her mom gulped down the last sip and poured out a second glass. "I think we deserve a second. It's happy hour somewhere!"

Tessa finished her glass as well, and placed it down on the counter in front of her mom so she could fill it.

"We still have two more to go," she said as she looked exhaustingly at the mixer. "I don't know how Nana used to be able to do this and more all by herself. She really was a kick, wasn't she?"

"She was incredible," Tessa said, wiping her top lip.

Her mom clapped her hands and began scooping out flour from the large bag on the counter. "Well, break's over! Let's get back to it."

Tessa groaned and started to remind her mom how she felt about baking, before returning to the counter to help. Looking down at the cookbook in her hands, she smiled. Maybe it was the smell of cookies baking in the oven, or the handwritten recipes, or the memories of making the book together, but despite a near-argument with her mom, Tessa felt a bit of a weight lift from her shoulders. It was good to be home baking cookies with her, even if they did bump heads a bit. Jay could have been onto something—maybe she had forgotten about all the tiny magical moments that made up the holiday season. She looked up at her mom who seemed so genuinely happy as she mixed the dough, and she was happy to be home.

Chapter 7

Though exhausted from a full day of baking, Tessa's mom convinced her to take a ride with her downtown to drop off a plate of cookies at the community dinner. Each year, Chestnut Ridge would host families in need for a special holiday meal at the community center. It was the first of many smaller celebrations that the town held leading up to its tree lighting and pageant. Her nana loved to get involved in the town groups that organized the Christmas events, and she was never too tired or busy to help plan or drop off a tray of food. Her nana believed in community and loved that, though we're in an age where the draw of a small town seems to be out of style, Chestnut Ridge held onto its roots.

Tessa insisted that her mom at least allow her to freshen up since she was covered head to toe in flour and desperately needed a shower. Her mom said she'd wait no longer than a half hour, which didn't leave enough time for her to wash her hair, but it would do. She didn't want to be caught off guard again after her morning with Chase.

Feeling much choosier with her outfit selection, she pulled on straight-legged jeans and a white top which she dressed up with a red and gold scarf, looped loosely around her neck. After running a brush through her hair and putting on small, gold hooped earrings, she ran back down the stairs to help her mom get the trays of cookies into the car in just the amount of time she promised.

Grabbing a tray from the table, she walked out into the garage and stopped in the doorway. "What? I just wanted to put on different clothes, you know, in case I bumped into anyone."

"*Mm-hmm . . .*" Her mom eyed her up and down.

"Oh stop, would you? I just didn't want to get caught again in a ratty old sweaty." Tessa pushed past her mother and dropped the cookies onto the backseat of her car.

"Is this your 'I made it' outfit you spoke so highly about?" her mom chirped, knowing it would push Tessa's buttons.

"No way! I need my power heels for that," she said returning the joking nature. "This is just my 'I was covered in flour and needed to freshen up' outfit."

"Whatever you say, Tessy! Get in the car before I show you my 'I hate to be late to the community dinner' outfit."

Rolling her eyes, Tessa walked around to the passenger side, slid into the seat, and secured her seat belt into the buckle. When her mom backed the car from the garage, she walked through the steps, stating it's always smart to check both your mirrors and turn to look before moving the car—all in good fun—teasing Tessa for her morning debacle.

Minutes later they were parked out front of the town hall. Tessa grabbed the two trays from the backseat of the car and followed her mom through the doors. Inside, a few of the women in town who were her mother's age raced to the door to snatch up the goodies and drop them off at the dessert table at the back of the room. Her mom reintroduced Tessa, sending the women into a five-minute fuss over how grown-up she was. After exchanging a few more niceties, they excused themselves to greet the next group, each of them saying how wonderful it was to have her back in town for the holidays.

Tessa looked around the room at the families sitting at the tables, each person seeming to have the slightest sign of hardship in their eyes. Year after year families were nominated anonymously by others in town to be selected for the dinner. Most of the time they were going through some sort of misfortune, either financially or emotionally, though it was never advertised what exactly each family was going through. Her nana always said that was the magic of it—you didn't have to wear your issues on your sleeve, but you could spend a night being catered to by your neighbors. The dinner was meant to be a relaxing night off, in an effort to bring some holiday cheer to those going through an otherwise gloomy situation.

Everyone else in town would volunteer to either bring food, drinks, or provide entertainment—anything to make the night special for those nominated. Tessa recognized her mom's large pot being brought into the kitchen, a saucy ladle dangling from the

115

side as most of it had been scooped out over a large bowl of pasta and placed at the end of the dinner buffet. She'd known her mom hadn't been cooking for just the two of them last night. She'd also known her mom wouldn't dream of showing up to the town dinner with just a few plates of cookies. Nana would be horrified with such a small donation, though it would have been seen as perfectly acceptable to everyone else.

Her mom waved at her from across the room to join her where she was standing. Quickly, Tessa tried to do a scan to see who the women were that her mom was chatting with, but she couldn't make out their faces with their backs turned. As she walked closer, she almost stopped in her path but thought better of it. Her mom was speaking with Jana, Tessa's childhood best friend and Ashley, Zak's wife.

Thankful that she had a chance to freshen up, Tessa made her way over to the group. Still a few feet away, Ashley opened her arms and gave her a tight hug, squeezing her as if they had been the closest of friends.

"It's so good to see you!" she said into her shoulder, away from where Tessa could see if she was being genuine or not.

Tessa pulled back. "You too." She smiled toward Jana whose face twisted into a smirk.

"I heard my husband was your *chauffeur* yesterday," Ashley said, bowing at the waist.

Tessa laughed awkwardly through her teeth. "And a fine one he was. Congratulations, by the way. I hear you have a lovely family."

"I know, crazy, right?" Ashley waved over at Zak and bounced a little from the ground. "He's just so cute, isn't he? I could squeeze him from here."

Nervously, Tessa shifted her glance to see who Zak was with and was relieved to see Mr. Flatts standing near, not Chase.

Interrupting Ashley's cheerful welcome, Jana said, "Good to see you too, Tess."

Picking up on Jana's vexation, she turned her attention back to the group. "I'm sorry, Jana, how've you been?" She moved into hug her, which Jana returned in a half-hearted way, barely wrapping a single arm around her.

"I'm great, how about you? City life everything you dreamed of and more?"

Tessa nodded yes, and began the well-practiced breakdown of her life.

Jana nodded, clearly not interested. Tessa didn't blame her. Jana was another person she'd left behind in Chestnut Ridge, despite having the type of decades-long friendship other girls at their school were jealous of. They were practically inseparable from kindergarten through their senior year, and each weekend they slept over at each other's houses, staying up late into the night talking about their dreams. When they were younger, Jana shared the same dreams, but after college, she moved back to Chestnut Ridge and had lived here ever since.

Up until then, the two of them had done everything else together, as planned, right up until they left for college. Jana and Zak had even dated for about half as long as her and Chase in high school, though based on her new friendship with Ashley, clearly everyone was over that. Jana didn't seem as quick to get over the end of the relationship between her and Tessa. When they each left for college, they promised they would call and visit, and for a while they did. But just like with Chase, eventually Tessa cut ties all together, finding it easier to stay away from Chestnut Ridge if she had nothing to go back to. It took some time, but Jana got the message as the majority of her calls and texts went unreturned.

After a lifetime of telling each other their deepest secrets, now they were struggling to get through the basics. Jana briefly touched on major life events, and Tessa's mom jumped in to point out that Jana and her husband bought a house just down the street from theirs about a year ago.

"I'm so happy for you, Jana. Sounds like things are going fantastic for you." She was happy for Jana—she believed she deserved the best.

"They are," Jana sneered. She excused herself from the group and offered a disingenuous, "Nice to see you."

Her mom tilted her head with a perceptive eye in Tessa's direction, proving the point that her actions weren't well received by all. Then she joined a conversation with another friend who was popping the cork from a bottle of a prosecco. Once poured, her mom handed a glass over and winked—she knew that reunion with Jana had been hard. For the second time today, they tapped their glasses, upgrading from milk to champagne, and toasting a sense of powering through.

As she sipped her bubbles, she took stock of who else she might know in the room, hoping to avoid being bombarded for a third time today. She caught Jana staring in her direction, who quickly looked away when she was caught. Brian, her husband and another Chestnut Ridge lifer, wrapped an arm around her and put a sweet kiss on the top of her head, clearly trying to comfort his steaming wife.

Suddenly feeling warm herself, Tessa set down her drink and walked through the double doors and into the corridor of the building before pushing open the last door between her and the exit. She didn't have her jacket, and the air outside was crisp and nipped at her skin, so she decided against getting the much-needed fresh air. Instead she moved off to the side near the Christmas tree that had been set up for the party by a group of younger children in town.

She'd been in Chestnut Ridge for almost twenty-four hours and had managed to bump into two people she'd hoped she wouldn't see. She pulled out her cell phone and accessed her calendar, wondering what she would've had scheduled if she was back in her element in the city. Scrolling over the next two weeks, the calendar was blank through January third. Ben must have had Andy clear it, knowing she would have a hard time keeping her input out of the countless meetings and events blocked into her schedule. Especially the meeting for the next day with Jay's

Jewelers. Never had she felt so disconnected from her life or who she was, and never had her calendar looked so bare.

"Someone's getting what they want for Christmas this year."

Tessa looked up to see Chase standing over her, two cups of prosecco in hand. "Excuse me?"

"Looks like someone's getting quite the present this year." Realizing Tessa still was not putting two and two together, he said, "You're sitting under the tree? Get it?"

"Oh!" she said with a laugh. "I get it—I'm the present."

Shrugging it off, Chase was now standing next to her. "Cheesy, I know. Sounded better on the walk over here to be honest, but hey, I gave it my best shot."

"Ah, gotcha . . . sounded good on paper, not in delivery."

Chase grinned and handed her one of the plastic flutes before sitting down next to her. They each took a sip, flirting with an awkward silence that thankfully Chase broke. "I didn't expect to see you here tonight. If I had, I would have mentioned it earlier at the market."

"I wasn't planning on coming, but my mom needed help dropping off the results of my forced labor."

Chase snickered. "Forced labor? Sounds intense."

"I've been baking Christmas cookies since I left you in the parking lot this morning. I'm still trying to figure out how Nana did it for all those years. We made ten or so batches, and I feel like I could sleep for a week."

"Nana's cookies are in there? Well, now I'm happy I showed up."

Tessa turned to face him. "You remember her cookies?"

"Not just her cookies—I loved eating anything over at your house. Everything was always unbelievably tasty. Even the veggies, which you know . . . veggies are veggies."

"Well, she really was something else in the kitchen, wasn't she?" Tessa said, remembering now just how often Chase had come over for dinner. His mom was lovely, but she mostly served up frozen lasagnas or occasionally grilled a burger. Nothing compared to the dinners at Tessa's house.

"Those were some good times back then," Chase said, trailing off at the end.

Tessa took a sip of prosecco and nodded in agreement. It was those good times that she stopped herself from thinking about. It's easier not to miss something if you don't think of it at all.

Chase gulped down the remainder of his drink and stood. "I'm happy I came tonight." He held out his hand and pulled her up to her feet and in close to his chest. Tessa snuck a look up to meet his eyes before taking a step back, her hand still in is. "I wasn't going to, you see. I'm not big on charity, but . . ." He paused as his kissed her hand like an old-time movie. "I got to see you, so I'll take it."

Tessa beamed. "What do you mean, charity?"

Releasing her grip, he ran his hand back through his hair, brushing it from his face. "I was chosen to attend this year because my mom's passing and all. Guess someone felt sorry for me being alone at the holidays. But you know how I am, I don't like people doing things for me. I'd rather be the one who's doing."

Even at a young age he was full of pride—she couldn't have imagined him being comfortable with people feeling sorry for him. Grown now, he was the prime example of a self-made, self-paid American man, never looking for handouts or assistance. And expressing his emotions was one of the only things he wasn't good at. It's how she knew she could get away with breaking up with him over an e-mail. He would never beg for her to reconsider; he would never want to come off as needy, and she took advantage of that back then. She made it easier on herself because if he begged, she would have gone weak at the knees and hopped on the first bus home to make it up to him. Even today, years later with a life so different from the one she had then, she didn't think she could say no face to face.

"I'm sorry, Chase, about your mom. Must've been really hard on you."

He shook his head and mumbled, "It was." With a quick swipe at his eyes, it was clear he didn't want her to see how he really felt.

Tessa placed her drink on the ledge, then wrapped him in a friendly embrace. She leaned back and met his eyes with all she needed to say, before squeezing his shoulders one last time.

"I see you two found each other!" her mom called across the room as she walked over.

Tessa backed away from Chase, picked up her drink, and finished it before walking toward her mom and the dinner.

"Chase, you gonna come in and get some food or sit out in the corridor all night?"

Following behind Tessa, he said, "Was just on my way in now, Ms. Gee."

"Well then, you better get in there. You're going to miss out on my sauce if you don't move it."

"I wouldn't want to miss out on that infamous sauce." Chase leaned in and gave her mom a quick kiss on the cheek as he passed. "Good to see you, Ms. Gee."

Her mom clasped Tessa's hand, squeezing it as they walked back into the room where the main dinner was being held. The crowd now felt a touch less uninviting.

Tessa skipped the buffet line and walked over to the table where the desserts were on display and snagged a cookie—she spent all day baking them, so she figured she deserved one. She watched as Chase made a heaping plate and grabbed a second glass of prosecco from the tray before sitting down next to Zak, who looked in her direction before whispering something close to Chase's ear. Chase lifted his eyes, and without lowering the fork from his hand, he glanced in her direction. His mouth formed into a trace of a smile before he returned to Zak and his food. Across the room, she bit into her cookie, grabbing a second one before she walked over to her mom.

Excusing herself for intruding in the table's conversation, she asked if her mom was okay to get a ride with one of the neighbors, explaining it had been a long day, and she was looking forward to getting back to the house.

A friend of her mother's, Deirdre, chimed in that she would be happy to drive her home before her mom could interject. After a fleeting effort to ask her to stay, she handed over the keys, jingling them slightly before dropping them in her hands. Tessa picked up her jacket from the rack at the front of the room, paused momentarily, and looked over her shoulder to steal one more glance at Chase before she left, trying to pay no heed to the feeling building in her chest, after seeing him again.

Chapter 8

Once in the car, Tessa started the ignition and turned the heat, still blasting cool air, up as high as the knob would turn. Even with a jacket and scarf she was freezing. Chestnut Ridge had the type of cold air that lived in your bones and froze you from the inside out.

Not wanting to make the same mistake again, she put the car in reverse and cautiously looked over both shoulders before beginning to back out of the space. On the passenger side of the back seat, she saw a plate stacked high with cookies and wrapped in a clear green plastic. She thought about running them into the community dinner but decided against it, wanting to avoid getting drawn into another conversation.

Once out of the space, she decided she would drop them off at Mr. Weaver's house, as a simple peace offering for hitting his car today and, what had seemed to be worse, making him miss his shows. Turning right at the end of the parking lot, in the opposite direction from her home, she started toward where she hoped he still lived. His house was run-down with an overgrown lawn that was littered with tools and things that probably held a purpose years back, but now they just sat. She assumed men like him didn't move often and that he'd also probably be home at this hour.

When she pulled up his driveway, she could see the television flickering in the front picture window of the otherwise dark house. Glancing down at the clock on the dashboard, she saw it was just after seven, and decided it was still a reasonable time to drop something off at someone's home unexpectedly.

As she walked up the front path, the irony in her life was hard to ignore. Two days prior, she would've never dropped off a plate of Christmas treats at a neighbor's home after a rude interaction—frustrating encounters were the norm in New York. The city may be a lot of things but neighborly was not one of them. People there barely had the oven space in their miniscule kitchens to bake Christmas cookies, let alone the kindness to drop them off next door. In New York, you lived in your own bubble, unaware of what those you shared a building or a sidewalk with were going through. Whether this was due to the sheer number of people who lived there or the type of people who flocked to the city's streets, New Yorkers rarely got caught up in the kind nuances of daily living.

Once at the front door she rang the bell and peaked back through the window to see no movement from Mr. Weaver's chair. Ringing the bell a second time, she heard a struggle and a begrudging mumble from the other side of the door.

Mr. Weaver creaked open the door, leaving just a few inches. "What are you doing here?"

Tessa extended the plate of cookies toward him. "I wanted to drop off some of my mom's homemade cookies as an apology for the trouble I caused you today. Not that it's an excuse, but I've only been back in town for a day and haven't driven a car in—I don't even know when the last time was—so it took me a second to get used to it. Sorry for any inconvenience it caused you . . ."

"I don't eat cookies. Never had a thing for sweets," he said, looking down at the plate.

Embarrassed by her failed attempt at a kind gesture, Tessa apologized for the intrusion, turned on her heel, and began to walk back down the front steps.

"Wait," Mr. Weaver grunted. "I'll take the cookies."

Pleased, Tessa skipped up the steps and handed them to him while attempting to wish him a happy holiday, but the door was already closed. She shrugged off a smile before walking down the path to her car, satisfied with her actions.

She even thought about texting Ben to tell him of her newfound Christmas spirit. Maybe he'd let her send a few e-mails if he thought his scheme was working. Through the window of the car she could see her phone in the center console, flashing with a text message across its screen. Throwing open the door, she shimmied her way in and grabbed the phone.

Hi, it's Chase. Hope it's okay that your mom gave me your new number.

She read over the text message again, considering how she should respond, when another message popped underneath.

You ran out of there tonight! I'd like to see you again . . . planned this time. No pressure, but if you want to meet for coffee tomorrow, let me know.

Tessa fixated on the screen, hoping he'd say more so she could avoid her turn to answer, but the three dots that signified someone typing never appeared. Her first instinct was to type in yes, that she'd love to, but she stopped herself to consider what having a coffee date with Chase meant long-term.

Chase, the person she left in Chestnut Ridge when she was eighteen because what they wanted was so drastically different. The same Chase she spent years trying to forget, dissolving their relationship to nothing more than puppy love. This wasn't her first time back in town, and the other times she'd made every attempt not to see him, staying in town for the shortest amount of time possible and barricading herself in her mom's house. She'd been fearful of the exact thing that had ended up happening this time—bumping into him and everything rushing back. Was it a good idea to start anything back up with Chase?

As she drove down the country roads, her mind kept going back to his text message and the consequences of her response either way. Tonight, standing next to that tree, the fire burning in the background, she could have wrapped herself up in his arms and stayed forever. Normally she'd blame the drinks, but she'd only had a few sips tonight. When he kissed her hand and pulled her in, her heart charged back to when she was younger and in love. There had been other dates and other guys in college, but one after the other seemed to fall short of making her feel the way she felt with him. So eventually she gave up. Part of the attraction was that Chase made her feel safe—most of her feelings stemmed from the fact that being with him was the only place she knew she could be herself, not some version others perceived.

There was no part to play or front to put on. With Chase, she could just *be*.

Back at her house she tried to distract herself by cleaning up the kitchen and pouring a glass of wine, but every few minutes she'd find a way back to her cell phone, clicking back into his text message. He'd like to see her for coffee. After a glass of cabernet, with a bit more liquid courage, she typed a message back.

Sure, I'd love to. It's just coffee ☺

After hitting send she waited anxiously for his reply, obsessing that she should have left the smiling emoji off. Thankfully, he was never one for games, and he wouldn't make her wait—she knew it. Within a minute he answered with a time and place, near the square, to meet. Offering the same courtesy, she quickly responded that she'd see him then.

Sitting back, more relaxed on the couch, she pulled a throw blanket across her lap and turned on the television to distract herself from overthinking the coffee date she'd just agreed to. She flipped through the channels until she found a Christmas movie and busied herself with other apps on her phone when it dinged again.

Thank you, Tess. Can't wait ☺

Her face lifted into a full-tooth grin as she said out loud to herself, "Looking forward to it."

"What on earth are you so happy about?" Her mom was standing in the doorway from the garage, untangling herself from her laced boots and scarf.

She shook the smile from her face and threw her phone to the other side of the couch. "Something tells me you might have an idea already, giving out my number at the community center and all."

Batting her eyes in a weak attempt at being coy, she said, "I can't imagine what I would have to do with it."

"You can stop with that weird look," she dismissed. "Chase told me you gave him my number, Mom."

"So? I didn't tell him to ask for it. He did all that on his own." She shook her arms and waist and cha-cha'd into the kitchen.

Following behind, Tessa asked if Chase had told her mom why he wanted her number.

Her mom filled the tea pot with water from the sink and lit the gas stove. "I'm assuming because he wanted to get in touch with you. He came over and asked where you ran off to, and I told him you went home. He seemed a little disappointed, like he wanted to talk to you more. So I told him you'd be in town through the holiday, and he asked for your number."

Leaning over the counter, Tessa ran back over what her mom said. "He seemed sad I left?"

"To me, yes." Her mom opened two tea bags and placed one in each mug. "Maybe after that moment I interrupted out in the corridor he had more he'd wanted to say. You two were getting quite cozy by the tree." She nudged Tessa with her hip.

"Mom, stop!" she said, swatting her away. "It wasn't like that. I told him I was sorry to hear about his mother, that I knew they were close, and he seemed like he could still be upset. So, I hugged him . . . to comfort him . . . That's all."

Her mom wrapped her arms around Tessa, mimicking her hug with Chase, and kissed her lovingly on the cheek. "You don't have to explain anything to me. It's okay to be happy, Tessy. And if hugging Chase makes you this happy, so be it."

Laughing, Tessa broke free from her mom. "I just don't want you to get any ideas in that head of yours. Just because I'm getting coffee with Chase doesn't mean that I'm picking up and moving back to Chestnut Ridge."

Her mom spun back, now facing her. "Coffee, huh? How adorably cliché," she said with her hands clasped in front of her heart.

"Mom!"

"Fine, fine. I get it, it's *just coffee*. You're not moving back, blah blah blah!" Her mom handed her the cup of tea, and Tessa graciously accepted it, holding the warm mug in both hands. She was still cold from the steering wheel a half hour earlier.

She sipped on the steaming liquid before saying, "It is pretty cheesy, isn't it? Come back to town, have your ex save you from a sticky situation, then ride off into the sunset—or the coffee shop, in my personal situation."

Her mom waved her hand, dismissing her question as she walked past her toward the living room. She sat down with one leg tucked under her on the couch. "Maybe, but sometimes— especially around the holidays—cheesy can be lovely, can't it?"

But Tessa was never one for cheesy. She hadn't had romantic clichés in her life since the time she'd spent with Chase. The men she dated in New York were all the same. All some sort of high-level executive, whether it be finance, business, or sales—dressed to a paragon in custom suits. They'd impress their dates with their knowledge of the wine list and speak of vacations they took to wine country or the beach—when they could get away from the office, of course. A solid date was one who would peel his eyes from his e-mail on his cell phone and hold a basic, polite conversation for more than five minutes. Rarely was any date planned from the heart rather than merely run in their formal business manner. After years of hoping for something as small as eye contact, and despite her best efforts to keep it casual, her heart fluttered at the idea of cheesy.

Chapter 9

After a restless night of sleep, Tessa woke early the next morning and did her best to pass the time until 10:00 a.m. when she was set to meet Chase. She decided it would be better to be a few minutes late—she wanted to avoid coming off as desperate and anxious to meet up with him. Her stomach cartwheeled as she walked down the freshly-shoveled sidewalk and up to the coffee shop window. Peering quickly through the glass, she could see Chase was already seated with a large coffee on the table in front of him. She always envied his confidence—it was one of the first things she'd noticed about him back when their friendship was still budding to romance. He was always comfortable in his own skin. If the table was turned and she'd arrived first, she would've taken a walk around the block or sat in the car, aimlessly scrolling through her cell phone—anything to not be seated alone in a booth waiting on someone.

She pushed open the glass door, ringing the bell that perched above the doorframe and alerting the few guests of the shop to look up from their coffees or pastries, most looking back down shortly after. Chase's face, however, lit up and remained focused on her as she approached the booth he was seated in.

Chase stood, leaned out of the booth, and kissed her cheek. "Good morning, you look stunning as usual."

Tessa looked down at her outfit choice, hoping it didn't come off as trying too hard. "So do you. Flannel always did you well."

Taking the good-natured jab in stride, Chase held out the flannel from his chest. "This old thing? Please. It's practically couture by now."

"Chestnut Ridge couture," she said, as she slid into the booth. "Never heard of that line."

A young waitress appeared, her name tag reading *Veronica,* to take her coffee order, and her tone was as lukewarm as the cup of coffee she brought over minutes later. Tessa's expectations for coffee were usually high, but when she asked for

143

almond milk and the response was that they didn't carry that flavor, she was reminded that here the choices were limited and anything would do.

As Veronica left the table, Chase watched Tessa stir in sugar, trying to mask her wish for a latte. "I'm happy you said you'd meet me. It was good to see you yesterday."

Tessa agreed. "I should be treating you to coffee after you helped with the situation with Mr. Weaver. I'd probably still be down at the market arguing with him over the lack of damage if it wasn't for you."

Chase leaned back, pushing both hands against the booth's table. "Eh, it was nothing. You looked pretty flustered, so I thought I'd jump in to give you a hand."

Tessa mumbled in agreement as she took a sip of her coffee, trying not to turn her nose up to the weak blend. The Roasted Nut, which she presumed was an attempt at a clever twist on the town's name, certainly wasn't a city coffee shop. But in a town where there wasn't even a drive-through chain, she knew the bar was set low. Chestnut Ridge was the type of place where the people were happy just to have something—it didn't have to be the best.

"So you haven't really said much about you. Still liking the big city?"

Clearing her throat, she stumbled around her words. "Well, it's . . . you know . . . it's great." She could kick herself for not being able to think of a better adjective other than *great* to describe her perfectly-planned life that she'd worked so hard for.

And it seemed Chase wasn't going to let her off that easy. "What's so *great* about it? Tell me more. I want to hear all about what you've been up to the last ten years."

Tessa sat forward, leaning an elbow on the table, her fingers nervously tapping at the weathered covering. "It really is great. I've been working at the same firm since I interned there in college, which sounds completely mundane, I know . . ." She paused to read his reaction. "But it's been a wonderful opportunity, and I've been able to move up fairly quickly. I'm a director now and work on the biggest campaigns, which means I get a lot of exposure in the industry. Obviously, that's ideal. I have a small team under me and a crazy, bouncy, twenty-two-year-old assistant who's a millennial to a tee, but very helpful."

"And is that all you do up there? Work?" he asked, interested but not as impressed as she'd hoped.

Tessa forced a smile. "Sometimes it does feel like that," she said as she tucked her hair behind her ears. "But let's see . . . I have a nice size apartment for New York. It's on the smaller side for anywhere else, but it's in an awesome neighborhood with delicious restaurants and bars. And—wait for it—I have a washer and dryer *inside* my unit. I know that might not seem like a big deal to you, but having a place by yourself and not having to pay to get your laundry done is like the definition of making it in the city."

"Whoa, Miss Tessa Gee," Chase jeered. "You are truly something. Can you really wash your own clothes in your own small-but-not-too-small apartment?"

"It sounds lame here in Chestnut Ridge where you can get a four-bedroom house and an acre of land for a few hundred thousand, doesn't it?" She forced her eyes to stay on his, not wanting to come off like she cared that he was judging her.

"Just a little," he said, grinning. "Regardless, I'm happy for you." Reaching across the table, he silenced her twittering fingers and held her hand in his. His thumb moved faintly across the top of hers. His smile faded at the corners, and Tessa could see through his eyes what he was thinking. She jerked her hand from his and fumbled with the side of the paper place mat. "What about you? Zak told me that things have been going pretty well for you. That you have your own business . . . That's something to be proud of."

Leaning back to his side and regaining his composure, he stirred his coffee. "Business has been good, and nothing beats being your own boss. Trends are showing that more and more people are moving out from the crowded suburbs, looking for a little more space, I guess to raise families. So there's been a good amount of demand for new construction. It's kept us busy." The bell above the door rang, and he lifted his hand to say hello to whoever entered. "Maybe it's the draw of having your own laundry room."

Her eyes narrowed into a stern look. "Ha ha! I know you're making fun of me, and I don't care." She sat back, arms crossed at her chest, before she allowed her breezy demeanor to return. "Being your own boss—I bet that's really wonderful. You can schedule your own day, not have anyone to answer to."

Chase pushed his hair from his face, laughing off how easy she made it sound. "There are a few perks, like I get to have coffee with you in the middle of the day. But most times it can be a real drag. You have no one to share the responsibility with."

"I can see that. Look at us all grown up," she said with a faint smile, the following silence prompting them to pick up their mugs and each take a sip.

"I can't say that I haven't enjoyed seeing you around. My visits to the market are usually much less entertaining."

"I think this is the first time that I'm back in town for more than twenty-four hours. Honestly, my boss forced me to use up my paid time off." Realizing how that must sound, she corrected herself. "He thought it would be good for me to take a breather at the holidays, start next year off with a fresh mind. So . . . here I am. Back home in Chestnut Ridge for two weeks."

"Your mom must really love your boss then. I can tell she misses you."

Tessa looked down at the table. "She doesn't exactly know that was the reason I came home. I felt weird making it seem like it wasn't my idea, so I said that I had the time off for once and was able to make it back home."

Chase nodded, not wanting to pry, and finished the last sip of his coffee. "I'm all out," he said, tipping the mug forward. "Probably time to get going anyways. Don't want to waste your entire day here with me."

"You're not wasting my day, and I have half a cup left."

He pulled a ten-dollar bill from his wallet and laid it out on the table. "I hope this isn't weird of me to ask, but Zak and Ashley are having a holiday party on Saturday—one of those parties where you wear a tacky Christmas sweater. Would you want to go with me?" Tessa didn't respond right away, so he jumped to downplay the invitation. "I'm assuming after a few days you'll probably be bored at home and looking to get out for a bit."

Tessa pulled another ten from her wallet and placed it on top of his, but Chase brushed it away. "It's just coffee, Tess. I insist."

"Well, if you insist," she said, sliding the bill back with the tip of her finger before tucking it back into her wallet. "I'll get you next time." If there was a next time.

"What about the party? Are you avoiding my invitation? Maybe I should insist on that too . . . I hate showing up alone to these things. Everyone else is married around here, and then there's me."

But she didn't believe his explanation for a minute. "I don't buy that, Chase. You've never cared about stuff like that."

He threw up his hands, palms-out in the air. "Fine, I've been caught. I was just hoping you'd want to go with me."

Coffee was one thing, but showing up at a party with your ex-boyfriend was another. Something like that would definitely get people talking in a town like Chestnut Ridge, but more time with him did sound like fun. "You sure Zak and Ashley would be okay with that? I haven't talked to most people here in years. I don't think they'd want an outsider like me at their party."

"Don't be silly, you're no outsider. And they'd absolutely be fine with it. It was Zak's idea. Called me after he dropped you off and said I should invite you."

Tessa took the last sip of her coffee before standing and pressing out the wrinkles in her blouse. "Sure, it could be fun. But I'll meet you there."

"You sure you don't want me to pick you up?" Chase asked.

Tessa was quick to answer. "I wouldn't want to get my mom all excited and have her thinking this was a date. You remember what she was like."

"I do." He extended his arm in an *after you* motion and followed her up the aisle between the tables and toward the door.

Once out on the sidewalk, she turned to face him. "Then I guess I'll see you Saturday."

"Yes, see you Saturday. It's a non-date," he teased, taking one step backward, still facing her before turning and continuing down the sidewalk. "Have a good one, Tess."

"Thanks for the coffee!" she yelled after him.

He spun on his heel with a wave, then continued back down the street. It wasn't until she saw him turn the corner that she let her shoulders drop and allowed her smile to grow from ear to ear. Despite the freezing temperature, her cheeks blushed to a Christmas red, and she found herself unable to deny that she was more excited about her non-date with Chase than any of her real dates in the city. Sitting with him took her back ten years, when every word that came from his mouth made her melt. Many times, she felt like she was the luckiest girl in their high school. Chase was always polite and kind—everyone was drawn in by his demeanor. She'd stand back as he talked with friends in the hall, watching him, wondering why he chose to be with her out of all the other girls. He'd find her in any crowd and glance at her in his adoring way, like he only had eyes for her. She knew they were young and that things would change, but back then, nothing made her happier than being by his side. And today, sipping on her subpar coffee, she was reminded of just how easy it was to be with him.

Chapter 10

Christmas music blared from her mom's wireless speaker as she walked through the door and into the kitchen. Her mom was bent over, rummaging through one of the cabinets, swaying her hips to "Up on the Rooftop." Nana's recipe book was open to her homemade hot chocolate recipe, which was likely the explanation for why her mom was shoulders-deep in the baking cabinet searching for the cocoa powder that was stored near the back.

"Making hot cocoa?" she asked, startling her mom.

She jumped up, just missing her head on the counter. "You scared me, Tessy. I didn't hear you come in the door."

Tessa picked up the tablet from the counter and lowered the music. "How could you hear anything with your carols blasting like we're at a rock concert?"

Her mom sashayed across the kitchen, her arms waving above her head, before raising the volume even higher than she originally had it. "I'm getting into the holiday spirit, because *we,*" she said, pointing at Tessa, "are going to cut down our very own Christmas tree today."

"Seriously?" She doubted the two of them could even carry the ax. "The two of us are going to cut down our own tree? Now that's a funny picture."

"We used to do it all the time! Don't tell me you've forgotten all those years we went down to the Breakridge Farm and spent hours searching for the perfect tree, all while drinking our thermos of tasty homemade hot chocolate. We'd take at least three loops around the lots trying to pick the best tree."

"I remember Nana snagging someone every year at the last minute to do the actual chopping."

Thinking back, her mom said, "That's true, but who needs 'em? We got this."

"Aren't we a little old for that now? I wouldn't want you to throw out your back trying to tie it to the roof of the car." She clearly lacked her mom's enthusiasm.

"Nonsense! Now read me that recipe for the hot chocolate. I'm still plenty young—we're going to cut down ourselves a tree."

Nana's recipe for hot chocolate was one she didn't need to look up in the book—she knew it by heart. She flipped to the page anyway, passing her hand over the drawing she'd made back in grade school of a steaming cup of cocoa surrounded by tiny red and green hearts that covered every spare inch of the page.

Unlike many other recipes, her nana's hot chocolate wasn't just for the Christmas season. With Nana, good and bad memories alike were sealed with a cup of cocoa. Whether it was warming up after a fun day with friends skating on the lake, or to comfort her as she lay with her head in Nana's lap because she and Chase had had a fight, her nana always had a cup ready for her when she needed it most. Many times, Nana would be having her nightly cup of tea and she'd peek in Tessa's room, pull her away from homework, and ask her to come have a cup with her. Being that she was so young, and hated the taste of decaffeinated green tea, Nana would whip her up a frothing cup of cocoa topped with whipped cream so smooth and creamy, it was as decadent as a dessert.

On special nights, she'd even pull down her china tea set from the top shelf of the cabinet over the refrigerator and dust out two cups and saucers. She'd look at the tiny cups with their exquisite floral patterns. "Tonight," she'd exclaim as she stirred the cocoa, "we can feel like two classy ladies, having high tea." And she'd fill each cup to the brim. Much to her nana's amusement, when the china set was out, Tessa would always sit up a little straighter and hold her pinky out like she'd seen on television. It was nights like these that she'd tell her, "Tessy, you can be anything you want to be. That's what makes us different than the animals and the plants. We can always change our place in life. Never let anyone tell you that you can't do something because I promise you, it's the best kept secret, we really can do whatever makes us happy in this life. We can work to get what we want. And you, my little Petunia, are going to be something truly special." Tessa would put her lips down into the whipped cream and come up with a chocolate-and-cream-laced smile at the thought of it. It was Nana who first let her believe she could leave Chestnut Ridge one day and do something more out in the world. She'd tell her to dream big, then bigger, and to never let anyone tell you not to.

The life lessons and her nana's cocoa recipe were ingrained in her—she could recite it in her sleep. One third a cup of cocoa powder, half a cup of sugar, three cups of milk, one cup of heavy cream, a dash of vanilla, and lastly—Tessa's favorite ingredient—two pinches of a coarse sea salt. Then she'd whisk it constantly so the milk wouldn't curdle, and when the mixture was steaming—not boiling—Nana would pour it into a mug, hold it with both hands, close her eyes, and say, "Now you just add a little bit of love."

"Do you remember the final step?" she asked her mom as she poured the cocoa out into two large travel mugs for them to bring with them to the farm.

"How could I forget?" She closed her eyes. "A little bit of love."

***

Two hours later they were on their third lap around the plots of Christmas trees at Breakridge Farm, debating between one tree that had a perfect shape but may be too wide for the house, and one that was narrow but tall. Tessa had to remind her mom that the tree always seemed larger once in the house, but her mom was on the hunt for something big and magnificent. Most years they found themselves back home with a monstrous tree that extended well into the center of the living room, but her mom always insisted that was half the fun, saying, "Christmas is the one time of year where the bigger, the gaudier, the louder, the more outrageous, the better."

"I think we should go for the wide one. We have the space for it in the room, even if it reaches the center." Her mom pointed toward the bottom of the well-shaped tree. "It's nice and full. I don't see any holes or dead spots. There's nothing I hate more

160

than when you have a big empty space right in the middle of the tree."

Tessa circled the tree, giving it one more pass over. "Want to take one more lap and make sure it's the one we want? Maybe there's something smaller."

"Okay, let's be sure. I've got a little cocoa left anyway—we might as well finish it before we attempt to chop this big boy down."

"I think she's a girl," Tessa chimed in. "With a very wide bottom."

"Ha! I like it! Let's tag her so no one else picks it." Her mom tied on the red ribbon with their sloppily-written last name, finishing it in a bow. "That would be our luck. Someone would hijack our tree."

"After all our searching, I'd say that big bottom girl is probably coming home with us," Tessa said as they started down the next row of trees. She glanced back quickly to make sure the tag was visible.

"So are you going to tell me how coffee went with Chase this morning, or are you going to make me beg to hear?"

Sighing, Tessa smiled. "I knew you'd ask eventually. I was trying to see how long you could last."

"Hey! Ok, that's actually pretty funny," her mom mused.

"Yes, and if you must know, it was really pleasant. I'm happy I agreed to go." She wasn't just saying that to appease her mom—she was happy she'd agreed to go. Maybe a little too happy.

"It's great to catch up with old friends, especially the ones you were as close with as Chase."

"We weren't just friends. Which makes things a bit more complicated. I didn't think I'd ever agree to open up that door again, but when I saw him at the dinner . . ." She trailed off. "He just seemed so lonely."

Her mom wrapped an arm around her shoulders, squeezing her. "There's my kind-hearted and compassionate Tessy! I knew she was in there somewhere under all that city smog."

"Mom . . ." she said, feeling less annoyed by the city jokes than she had a few days ago.

"Jokes aside, losing a parent is extremely difficult. I know— I was heartbroken when we lost Nana. There's a void that nothing or no one can fill."

Lately, Tessa regretted leaving her mom so quickly after her nana's funeral. "I'm sorry I had to rush back to work after that. Looking back, I probably should've stuck around for a few days and helped you adjust."

"Oh, hush!" her mom said. "I'm not serving you up a guilt trip. I just think that Chase is probably grateful for the distraction."

"He did invite me to Zak's Christmas party tomorrow. Some kind of ugly Christmas sweater party. I've never even heard of such a thing."

Her mom elbowed her. "You didn't tell me that. How delightful! Do you have an ugly Christmas sweater?"

Tessa hadn't thought of that. Most people who paid top dollar for a Manhattan zip code preferred swanky top-floor Christmas parties, not making a fool of themselves by wearing a dated, ugly Christmas sweater.

"Well then," her mom said, "we'll have to pick this tree and get on home! We're going shopping in Nana's trunk. You know that lady loved herself a bedazzled sweater."

It was true, Nana loved dressing up for every holiday, Christmas being no exception. For the entire month of December, she'd don gaudy sweaters and flare, as she called it—jingle bell necklaces or ornament earrings. When she was young, she'd thought Nana was nothing but cool for all her glitter, but as Tessa grew older, she'd become embarrassed of her outrageous outfits. But Nana never cared. She would scold her, saying you were never too old to have a little fun.

They moved quickly through the last row, now having to get home. "You saved all that stuff?"

"Not all of it. I couldn't let some of my favorites go, though."

Tessa understood. Nana had a few outfits that were her staples. There were many emotions tied to those sweaters. "Then shopping in Nana's trunk it is! Let's go cut down this tree."

Her mom clasped her hand, squeezing it three times—their sign for 'I love you'—and they walked back up the plot toward the tree they'd tagged. Tessa reciprocated the gesture, tightening her grip in the same pattern as she tilted her head onto her mom's shoulder.

After a struggle with the saw and the help from a kind father of two, the tree was cut down and paid for. Despite the help they needed at the end, they felt they could say they got it mostly down on their own. Tessa sat on an old fence, the tree at her feet wrapped in netting, and waited for her mom to pull the car around. From the corner of her eye she saw Mr. Flatts handing out string to other purchasers who needed to secure the trees to the tops of their cars.

Tessa hopped down from the fence and stepped over their tree. "Mr. Flatts!" She waved as he turned in a full circle, looking to see who called out his name.

He stopped spinning once he spotted her. "Look who it is— Tessa Gee." A longtime friend of Nana's, Mr. Flatts was the kind of older man who always had candy in his pocket to share or would pull a quarter out from behind your ear.

"How are you holding up?" she asked. "If you're still out here helping with the tree farm, I'd say you must be doing pretty well."

Chuckling, he wrapped the excess string into a loop around his forearm. "You know me, I like to get out of the house. How's your family? Mom doing well?"

Tessa nodded. "Very well. She's happy to have me home for a bit."

"I bet she is. You better tell her that her cookies were fantastic at the dinner. May not have been your Nana's, but they were darn close!"

"That's an honor!" she joked. "We baked those together."

"Your nana . . . boy was she one heck of a cook. I asked her to marry me every day, but she always told me she was a one-man lady. She loved your grandfather, even after he was gone."

Tessa swooned at the thought. She never knew her grandfather, but Nana did wear her silver wedding band each and every day, taking it off only if she was elbows-deep in raw dough or rolling meatballs. He'd passed when she was too young to remember, but she knew Nana loved him. Though it didn't stop her from arguing with him, even after he was gone. She'd announce to Tessa and her mom that she was angry with him over some event from their past, and her mom was always quick to point out that he wasn't exactly around to defend himself. Nana would scoff and say something like, "Heck, who knows where I'd be if he hadn't been afraid to spend a single penny. I could be eating a baguette at a bistro in Paris." Neither she or her mom would dream of reminding Nana that she refused to fly on airplanes—there was no use. She'd drag on about her fantasy scenarios regardless. Her mom chalked it up to Nana's way of keeping in touch with him.

The car pulled up, and her mom rolled down the window to smile and say hello to Mr. Flatts as he approached. "Think we can grab some of that string? Silly me, I left ours in the garage."

"That's what I'm here for! Everyone forgets the string," he said as he began unraveling what he had just looped from his arm.

168

Between the three of them, they managed to tie the tree to the top of the car. "This beauty ain't going nowhere." Mr. Flatts backed up to take one final look over their work.

"Told you we got this, Tessy. And you thought we were too old," her mom said as she rounded the car and sat back in the driver's seat. Tessa opened the passenger side and stepped one leg up into the car.

"Hey, Tessa!" Mr. Flatts yelled after her. "I know you are a busy gal, but we can always use some help with the dinner for the night of the pageant and tree lighting. Your mom's down for a tray of penne a la vodka already, but if you'd like to get involved, we can always use more food or someone to help organize the drop-offs the day of."

Tessa thought of her nana, making tray after tray of food for the tree lighting, then bossing the other ladies around as she orchestrated the perfect holiday potluck. She'd become the self-proclaimed event manager. "I'd love to. Where can I sign up?"

"Why don't you just come in early that day. Your mom always likes to be first with her food anyway. You can help me set up and organize the other stuff as it comes in. How does that sound?"

"Perfect, see you then," Tessa said, swinging her other leg into the car. "Stay warm, Mr. Flatts, and don't work too hard out there!"

The wheels spun in the snow as her mom pulled away, and Tessa glanced up through the clear sunroof to check on the tree.

Her mom, eyes still on the road, said, "I was shocked to hear you say yes to helping with the pageant."

Reaching across the center console, Tessa turned the volume down on the radio. "It's not a big deal. I know how much the pageant meant to Nana, so I thought it would be nice to get involved. Plus, you're going to be there all day—what else am I going to do, knit a sweater?"

Her mom laughed out loud and said, "I'd like to see that one—you knitting? Now that's funny." It took her a minute to settle from her fit before she could continue. "In all seriousness though, Tess, she'd be honored that you're getting involved with the pageant and so, so proud of you."

Turning her attention out the window and onto the passing trees, she hoped her mother was right.

Chapter 11

Tessa typed the words "ugly Christmas sweater party" into the search bar of her browser and was bombarded with pages of results, one photo splashier than the next. Either her crowd in the city didn't throw these types of parties, or Tessa had been living under a rock to not have noticed the absurd trend. Grown adults, wrapping themselves in tinsel, dressed in outfits made from Christmas bows and packaging, or men wearing sweaters with stuffed animal-like reindeer heads popping from the chest. There seemed to be an entire market that catered to the over-the-top party theme. Not only could you purchase a hideous sweater from the internet if you weren't the crafting type and had a spare forty dollars to blow, but there was also a decent selection of décor, tableware, favors, and recipes to fit the theme. When she scrolled across the twenty-dollar ugly sweaters for pets, she closed her laptop—there was always a point in the never-ending search results where it had gone too far.

She went back down to the kitchen, and her mom handed her a cup of coffee.

"Am I the only person in Chestnut Ridge who has never heard of an ugly Christmas sweater party? I seriously had no idea this was a thing." She was still partly in shock at the popularity of the idiotic concept.

Passing the milk across the table, her mom said, "What's there to hear about them? As far as I know, you wear an old, hideous sweater—you know, the kind that a weird aunt or uncle would wear to Christmas dinner." Somehow, her mom seemed more in the know than her.

"It's a huge thing apparently! People get creative and like . . . craft! They do DIY projects, and it's like, the more outrageous the better. They have ugly sweaters for dogs! Please tell me you agree that's pushing it."

Tessa's mom couldn't hold in her laughter while she assured her that there was no need to craft and that, luckily for

Tessa, her nana was the queen of outrageous sweaters. She was more than certain they'd be able to find something in her trunk that would fit the party's theme perfectly.

After a scaled-down breakfast of eggs and sausage—the real kind as her mom said, none of that turkey nonsense—the two of them pulled down the ladder that led up to the attic. They were soon surrounded by Nana's dazzling sweaters, finding it both ridiculous and amusing that she was apparently ahead of her time, spearheading the flashy trend decades prior to its burst into mainstream commercialism. Not only did her nana have sweaters for Christmas, but she had some accented with witches for Halloween and red, white, and blue sequined shirts for the Fourth of July. Though she was one hundred percent Italian, she also had a handful of green shamrock frocks presumably for St. Patrick's Day.

Tessa wouldn't dream of dressing in such a ridiculous manner for a date in New York—a significant part of your self-worth in that city came from the price tag on your clothes or the designer's name on your handbag—yet for an evening with Chase, she was shopping for an outfit from Nana's old, musty trunk. As she sifted through the pile of sweaters, she reminded herself again and again that this wasn't a date. Chase had simply invited her to a mutual friend's party and that just because the theme was foolish, it didn't mean she had to show up dressed like a fool.

She held up a black-and-red-plaid patterned sweater, the least loud of the options. "What do you think of this?"

"That's not an ugly sweater. There's not even a streak of glitter on it," her mom said, pulling the shirt from Tessa's grip. She held it up to her petite frame, the same one Tessa and her nana shared. "I think I'll wear this to the pageant, though. Looks like Nana never even took the tag off. You" —she pointed in Tessa's direction—"get looking for something in this pile with a little more pizzazz."

Tessa picked up one sweater at a time before shaking her head and tossing it over to her mom to fold and put back in the trunk. After rummaging through two thirds of the pile, Tessa reached for one she recognized and spread it out on the floor in front of her. Unlike many of the others, this sweater was cotton soft and black, Tessa's preferred color to dress in. In the center was a Nutcracker appliqué, carefully bedazzled with beads and sequins. Her nana wore it each year to Tessa's winter ballet recital—even the years her class wasn't performing *The Nutcracker*. She picked it up and held it to her face, catching the faintest whiff of Nana's powder-scented perfume. Turning the sweater toward her mother, she asked, "What about this one? Flashy enough for you?"

"I think it's perfect," her mom said. Her own memories of the sweater appeared to play across her face.

They picked up the remaining sweaters from the floor and placed them back in the trunk. Her mom shut the top and secured it closed. "Well, at least you know you have options for the next ten years of ugly sweater parties."

Tessa was going to correct her—remind her it would likely be the first and last party in Chestnut Ridge for a long time, but instead she paused at the thought of her and Chase, matching like some of the couples she saw online. Holding the sweater up one more time, she said, "Let's just start with one . . . see how it goes from there."

***

In the early evening, after pouring herself a glass of wine to calm her nerves, she stood in front of her floor-length mirror looking over her uncharacteristic outfit. She decided to wear a collared white shirt under the sweater, feeling a little more like herself in that style. Opting for minimal eye makeup but a bright red lipstick, she finished her look with her nana's pearl earrings. As she secured the backs onto the posts, she half-jokingly thanked Nana for letting her borrow her vintage things.

As she touched up her lipstick, wanting it to look just right, her phone pinged on her bed with a text from Chase.

Changed my mind, I'm picking you up. Does that make it a date? I'll be there in fifteen minutes.

Realizing he never sent her Zac's new address and that this seemed to have been his plan all along, she laughed under her breath and typed a response.

So sneaky . . . I guess it does. Text me when you're out front.

With one more glance in the mirror, she grabbed her smaller purse and glass of wine from the bedside table and made a promise to herself that the night was going to go fine, and she headed downstairs to wait for her ride.

Her mom was curled up on the couch, snugly tucked under her flannel blanket, eyes locked on a cartoon Christmas special that was much older than her. The clay figures marched across the screen as Tessa paraded in front of the television, swaying from side to side to the same rhythm, showing off her outfit. "So . . . What do you think? Am I ugly enough?"

Before she could answer, the doorbell rung, their attention now on the front door.

"I thought you said you were driving tonight, sweetie." Her mom kicked off her blanket and made a beeline for the door. Tessa shuffled after her, just turning the corner into the foyer as her mom swung open the front door.

Chase stood with his back to them before turning around, his eyes immediately locking on Tessa. For a moment they stood, staring back at one another, and her mom cleared her throat to remind them she was still there.

"Ms. Gee," he said, reaching to shake her hand as she pulled him in for a hug. He smiled at Tessa over her mom's shoulder before stepping back. "You look stunning, Tess."

"Oh, please!" she gushed. "I'm in an ugly sweater."

"Well, nothing could look ugly on you." He pulled her in, greeting her with a simple hug before turning back to her mom.

"Do I need to have her home before twelve like in the good ole days, Ms. Gee?"

Her mom smacked him lightly on his shoulder. "Don't you tease me. You two were kids then . . . You're all grown now. How about a quarter after?" she said sarcastically.

Chase played along. "A quarter after it is, and not a minute later."

"Ha ha, you guys are so funny," Tessa said as she slid her arms into the sleeves of her coat. She kissed her mom as she passed by. "Don't wait up . . . or do. Whatever you'd like."

Chase reached for her hand, helping her down the snow-covered steps before leading her down the front walk. Her mom watched from the doorway, a soft smile on her face.

Chapter 12

After a brief car ride filled with easy conversation, they pulled up to Zak and Ashley's house and parked along the side of the street with the other cars. The house was illuminated by colorful lights, with barely a dark square foot inside or outside the two-story home.

"You ready to head into the party?" Chase said, as he turned off the ignition.

Looking up at the dazzling house, her nerves heightened. It had been over ten years since she'd seen most of the partygoers inside—the same people who'd made her feel like she wanted to crawl out of her skin back in high school. The same people she thought she'd be better off leaving behind.

"Are you sure they know I'm coming?" she asked, attempting to swallow her insecurities.

"Of course they do. I just talked to Zak about an hour ago. He asked me to grab more wine," he said, motioning to the back seat and a partitioned, reusable shopping bag containing four bottles of red. "Apparently white is out of style. They have plenty of chardonnay left, but the pinot noir and cabernet were being poured like crazy."

"I think Chardonnay definitely went out of style a long time ago."

Chase picked up her hand in his. "Can we go inside, Tess? We at least have to bring in the wine. We don't want to be responsible for everyone switching over to martinis now, do we?"

"Now that is a scary thought." She gritted her teeth. "Married couples on candy cane martinis?"

"Oh now, that will happen anyway," he said. "You should see half these ladies after a martini."

"Let's get this over with, I guess." She unlocked the door and stood, taking one more look over the house. Chase rounded the car, joined his free hand with hers, and winked. Somehow it felt like he understood how she felt, despite the fact that she had left him too. An old sense of security came over her, and they walked up to the door hand in hand. She'd always felt safer when Chase was by her side.

Ashley answered the front door, decked out in red and green from her walloping red bow atop her head, all the way down to the green elf-style socks on her feet. After an enthusiastic welcome and a bouncing hug, she shooed them down the hall and into the large main area of the house. It had a far-reaching, open floor plan complete with an intricately styled kitchen, dining, and family room. Like Ashley and the outside of the house, the inside was bursting with Christmas colors and gold glitter—there were even crystal snowflakes hanging from the ceiling, sending shimmering specks of light around the large room.

Ashley led them from couple to couple, saying some version of, "You remember Tessa Gee? Yes, she moved away." Tessa nervously shook everyone's hand and exclaimed how great it was to see them, hoping they couldn't see through her confident exterior. Thankfully, Ashley was briskly moving them through the crowd, so she only spent a minute or so with each group.

As they made their way to the back corner of the kitchen, Zak yelled, "Look at this happy couple! What is this, 2006?"

Ashley scurried over, hushing him and waving her hands in the air, like the room didn't just hear what he said. "Zak here is going to make you one of his famous martinis to make up for that *rude*" —she said, poking him below the ribs—"comment."

Looking up at Chase, Tessa burst out laughing. "No, thank you—a little elf told me I should stay away from those." Ashley looked back at her, not understanding her use of the holiday phrase. "I'll just have a glass of wine if there's any left."

When it finally seemed to click, Ashley abruptly aimed her scolding at Chase. "Now, what did you tell Tess? It was only that one year when things got a little out of hand—the first year when all the kids stayed at their grandparents—can you blame us?" she said with a laugh. "He's revised the recipe since then. *Way* less alcohol."

Chase put up two hands to gesture his surrender. "I haven't said a thing, Ash."

She mumbled an *mm-hmm* and reached for a festive red-and-white wine glass that had buttons up the front mimicking a Santa suit.

Chase reached into the bag of wine and pulled out a California cabernet. "I took a guess, but I'm thinking a cab is your favorite."

Tessa nodded, trying to recall if she even drank wine until after college. She had posted a few bottles of her favorites on her limited social media. Maybe Chase checked in on her too.

After pouring her an appropriate amount, Chase grabbed a second glass—a similar style to hers but resembling an elf—and poured a glass for himself. "To Christmas miracles," he said, clicking his glass against hers. "I never thought I'd get you to wear an ugly sweater."

Looking down at the gaudy Nutcracker on her chest, her smile pulled in tight. "I thought you said it looked good."

Chase took a swig of his wine, and Ashley jumped to her defense. "I love it! He's just messing with you, these two . . ." She waved her hand toward Chase and Zak. "Always thinking they're so funny. But here's a clue: you're not," she finished with huff.

Tessa couldn't help but notice that Ashley seemed to be creating a foursome between the two of them and Zak and Chase, probably already planning double dates and couple game nights in her mind.

"You look great, Tess, really." Chase said clicking her glass again. "I'm just messing with you."

She took a long sip of her wine, hoping it would calm her a bit. As Chase excused himself with Zak, she skimmed the room, noticing that Jana sat on an upholstered chair directly across from where Tessa stood. She was chatting with another couple. When their eyes met, Tessa raised her hand, and Jana did the same, each sharing a closed-mouth smile. Tessa made a mental note to try to talk to her at some point during the party, but she'd give her space for now.

Still looking around the crowd in the room, she felt Chase grab her hand. He leaned in and whispered in her ear, "Let's hide for a second." He lightly pulled her down a hallway that led off the back side of the kitchen. "I want to show you my favorite part of the house. When we built it, I almost told Zak he couldn't have it, just because of this."

At the end of the hall he opened a sliding wood door to reveal a study with a rustic stone fireplace against one of the walls, the stones extending from floor to ceiling. In front of the fireplace sat two oversized chairs. "Shall we?"

"Was this your plan?" she asked with raised eyebrows. "To get me in Zak's study alone, just us and a romantic fire? How high school of you . . ." She walked past him, sat in one of the chairs, and crossed her legs.

"Never," he said, still on the other side of the room. "I just know you well enough to see that you were uncomfortable, and I thought you could use a break from your little reunion."

She couldn't argue with him there—it was more than the truth.

"Plus, I wanted to have a chance to catch up," he said, sitting down in the chair across from her. "I'm not gonna lie, I'd rather be in here with you then out there with everyone else."

They sat for a moment, slowly sipping their wine as the wood crackled in the fire. "I love that sound—that popping noise the wood makes in the fire. Up in the city, at restaurants and such, it's all gas fireplaces. That sound reminds me of when we used to have fires back at home."

"Do you miss it sometimes when you're up there? I mean, I get it, Chestnut Ridge is not much to speak of. But there must be some times when the city and how fast everything moves just gets . . ."

"Overwhelming."

"Overwhelming," Chase repeated.

"I didn't think it was getting to me. I didn't feel overwhelmed. But you forget how quiet the quiet can be, and how dark it gets at night without all the lights. The first night back in Chestnut Ridge I didn't know if I was going to sleep like a baby or be up all night from how quiet and dark it was."

"Well, which one was it in the end?" he asked, taking a sip.

She moved her eyes from the fire to his. "Slept like a baby."

Chase nodded in agreement. He seemed to understand.

"What about you, though? Does the quiet of this place ever get to you? Don't you ever want to see more?" Looking over at him, she could tell his answer before he spoke. He seemed confidently content.

"I can leave anytime I want—see something else, do something else. But any time I've left, I've always felt like I couldn't wait to be back. And after a while, I've just accepted that maybe Chestnut Ridge in all its unassuming glory is home for me."

"I suppose it's not that bad here. For so long I was focused on leaving, but for the first time in a while I've enjoyed the simplicity. It's relaxing not to have all the hubbub around you twenty-four seven."

Chase stood and moved to her side where he lowered himself to her eye level, his hand on the arm of the chair. He leaned in, eyes flickering from the fire. "It's been so good having you here."

"There you two are!" Ashley yelled, her martini in hand. "We just turned the music on, and I need you two to come dance with us. Everyone else is just sitting around."

Chase clearly didn't want to move his eyes from Tessa's. "We wouldn't want to miss that now, would we." He straightened his back and started for the door, and Tessa stood to follow. Ashley winked when Chase passed, then she grabbed Tessa's arm, holding her in the study.

"That was just super cute. I am so sorry!" She exaggerated her words with her animated hands. "I really hope I didn't just interrupt something."

"Absolutely not, we were just talking. Chase and I are . . ." she trailed off as she watched him walk down the hall and back into the party. Zak put a hand on his shoulder and led him back toward the drinks. "We've been over as a couple for a long time. We're just friends."

"You never know! It is Christmas after all, and anything can happen at Christmas. That's the magic of it!" She clapped her hands together before clasping them and holding them up to her face.

Tessa finished her wine in a single gulp before following Ashley who flitted back down the hall and into the party. She paused in the entryway to the kitchen and looked across the room, wondering what Chase and Zak were talking about. She hoped she wasn't misreading the situation that had almost just unfolded before they were interrupted by Ashley the elf. It seemed like Chase would have tried to kiss her. Maybe it was the fire or the Christmas magic that everyone around her believed in without question, but she knew she would have let him.

Ashley was now standing on the sofa, squealing for everyone to pipe down for her speech as she pointed the remote at the wireless speaker and cut down the volume of the cheery holiday tunes. For a tiny thing, she had a way of demanding attention.

Zak excused himself from Chase and walked to the front of the living area to stand next to his wife. Chase came to stand by Tessa and leaned on the opposite side of the doorframe.

Ashley thanked her guests for joining them and proceeded to point out some of her favorite themed outfits from the group in front of her. After applauding everyone for their ugly sweaters, and thanking Zak for his help with the decorations, she declared, "Now, let's party. I want to see everyone up and dancing! I'm serious! You all have three seconds to get off your seats." Zak wrapped his arms around her and hoisted her off the couch, holding her in the air and spinning before placing her down on the floor and landing a sweet kiss on her lips. As she watched them, Tessa couldn't deny that they looked happy together.

"You heard her. Trust me, I've tried to get out of dancing before—it's not pretty." Chase stretched his hand out to her and mockingly dipped into a bow.

"Is that so? I suppose we wouldn't want to upset a five-foot elf in a bow."

"That little elf over there" —he pointed in Ashley's direction—"she seems sweet, but you don't want to make her mad."

Tessa placed her hand in his and let him lead her to the area in the living room that was cleared for a makeshift dance floor. She tugged at his arm and motioned to go toward the back corner of the room, not wanting to be the center of attention in this particular crowd. Over his shoulder, Zak handed them their refilled wine glasses, and Tessa gladly accepted. Nothing called for a second glass of wine like a dance party with old schoolmates.

They each swayed to the upbeat melodies, getting mildly more comfortable by the chorus. By the second song, Chase reached for her glass and handbag and placed both on a shelf behind them. He then took her hands in his and waved them one at a time before releasing one to spin her into him, then back out, their arms extended.

"Since when do you know how to dance?" Tessa's tone was mocking, but she was half serious. Although he wasn't doing any technical moves, his rhythm had improved since their last attempt at the senior prom.

"Since never." He dipped her back in an exaggerated ballroom move. Tessa cracked up as he spun her around and posed.

"Baby It's Cold Outside" blasted through the speakers and Ashley squealed and began singing, acting out the verses while Zak followed along. "When is everyone going to accept that this song is totally creepy?" Tessa watched the performance.

"What!" Chase exclaimed. "It's just about the most romantic Christmas song ever."

"Have you actually listened to the words? The guy is a creep!" She looked around the room and sensed hers was an unfavorable opinion as the other couples were rocking together, singing the words.

Chase pulled her in closer, one hand clasped with hers, the other on her waist and whispered, "But baby, it's cold outside."

Shaking her head, she looked up at him and mouthed, "I ought to say no, no, no, sir."

He smiled and spun her around, her back to his chest as he moved right to left. His arm crossed loosely around her middle, hugging her close to him. "But baby," he sang, unable to hold it in, "It's cold outside."

She leaned her head back against his shoulder, giggling softly while he continued to sing along, and she eventually joined in with the female lines she knew. On the last verse, he unraveled her from his arms, knelt on one knee, and lifted his hand to her, belting the last line.

She clapped her hands, laughing as the music slowed.

As he stood, Tessa took a step into him and wrapped her arms over his shoulders and slowly swayed to "I'll Be Home For Christmas." The room tunneled around them, blocking out the noise and the other couples dancing. Tessa shook her head and sighed, taking an easy breath that turned to a smile as they moved to the music. She felt like there were so many things she could say, but decided not to muddle the moment and said nothing at all. Chase raised his hand to her cheek, brushing her hair behind her ears. Though they were leaned in close to each other, they both held back from taking the next step to get even closer. The song ended, but they remained still for a moment longer, arms draped freely around each other and staring into each other's eyes before they finally looked away and separated. Tessa turned toward the bookshelf and took a sip of her wine before reaching into her purse.

Inside, her phone was flashing with multiple messages from Ben. Like a punch to the stomach, she snapped back to reality. Anxiously, she entered her passcode, having to do it twice to view the messages. Panic quickly replaced the ease she was just enjoying with Chase. As she read the words in his text messages, the air seemed to leave her body. Jay's Jewelers was leaving the firm. This meant thousands of dollars of lost revenue, and Ben was blaming it all on her. The meeting on Friday did not go well, and apparently Jay more than expressed his opinions on their tired and lackluster creatives as of late. The firm's biggest client—her client, who she was usually quick to point out she managed mostly on her own—was leaving, and it was due to her creative concepts.

Suddenly feeling irritated by the loud party happening around her and the carefree couples, she grabbed her purse and rushed toward the front door. She ignored Chase who was calling after her, asking where she was going.

Without turning around, she replied in a harsher tone then she would have liked. "I just need a minute."

Out on the front porch, the cold air prickled her skin and she fumbled through her phone to find Ben's number.

"It's me," she said, nearly out of breath. "I just got your messages. What happened? When did you get the news?"

Ben huffed, clearly annoyed she made him wait. "I texted well over an hour ago. I know I said no e-mail, but you'd think getting a message like that would make you pick up the phone and call."

"I am so sorry—I'm out at a Christmas party and didn't have my phone on me." She hated the excuse and felt childish using it.

"The meeting was a disaster. Jay and his internal guys tore apart everything we've done for them the past few years. Forget the holiday campaign—they ripped apart everything, said they've been wanting to give the firm the benefit of the doubt. They were hoping it was some sort of slump, but the Christmas proposal was the final straw. They can't work with a team that can't capture emotion."

"Ugh!" She rubbed at her temple, which was now throbbing. "Did you really think the holiday campaign was that bad?" she asked, fearful of the answer. When he didn't answer immediately, she pressed harder. "You didn't say anything when I ran it by you. You actually said you liked it."

"Now, hold on. Did I think it was your best? No, but it wasn't the worst I've seen, that's for sure, and it was last minute. I wanted the extra revenue. If I'm being honest, it was a little dry, cold—however they said it—but it doesn't matter now. They want to walk, and it doesn't look like we're going to be able to stop them."

Tessa sat down on the steps, the feeling gone from her limbs. "They can't leave. They have a huge retainer with us. That would be . . ."

"Bad. Tessa, I know. Very bad."

"What are you going to do?" She felt even more like a child looking to an adult for the answer. Her mind ran through all the possibilities of how she could save the client, but she couldn't process anything that made sense.

"You're not going to like it, but I did what I had to do. I threw you under the bus—said you were overworked and needed a vacation. I personally offered to manage the account until things were back up to the standards they were used to. I don't know if that's going to do anything, but I had to try. They seemed to agree that your work has been suffering as of late. You did handle this one mostly on your own . . ."

Tessa's ears hissed. How could Jay think that? They seemed perfectly happy up until that last meeting. And Ben—how could he throw her under the bus that way? Was it his plan all along to make her take the fall? Was that why he had shipped her out to Chestnut Ridge? He wanted to make sure she wouldn't be there to disrupt his save tactic? "This wasn't all on me, Ben. You approved the presentation."

"Maybe not, but someone needs to go down for this and it has to be you. Without Jay's Jewelers, we may not be here next

Christmas." After everything she'd done for the firm the last few years, he was willing to sacrifice her.

Her eyes stung at the corners, and a lump was building in the back of her throat. Though she wholeheartedly believed that as a woman you should never cry in the workplace, she couldn't believe Ben had betrayed her. It was getting harder to swallow as the conversation continued. He signed off on all creative concepts. There wasn't a presentation that was pitched to a client that he didn't see first and approve. Yet when a client complains, he sits back in his chair with his hands up, placing the blame squarely on her shoulders, not considering his role at all.

"If I had been there, maybe I would have been able to save the situation, say something to Jay . . . We always had a great working relationship. I'm sure I could've gotten him to change his mind." She wanted to believe that, but she really wasn't sure.

Ben paused. "I don't think that would have been the case. They had some choice words regarding my decision to keep a creative director on staff who didn't know how to convey emotion. It's probably for the best that you weren't there."

Tessa stayed silent, not knowing what else to say. Everything she'd worked for seemed to be falling apart after one lousy meeting.

"Regardless, I wanted to keep you in the loop. They're going to tell us their new plan for the year by December thirty-first. I'm hoping that my promise to be involved in the day-to-day management of their account will help them choose to give it one more shot."

"And what about me?" Tessa asked.

"There's plenty you could do, Tess. We'll figure it out later, whatever the case may be. If I get an update from Jay, I'll call back." Ben didn't need to say it; she knew well enough that it wouldn't be good for her either way. Losing a top client was pretty much the best way to get demoted in her field. "And, Tessa, don't go firing off any messages trying to fix this. I need you to stay out of it for now."

After telling Ben that she understood, she hung up and allowed the tears she'd wanted to hold in slip down her face. Of all the places to receive a call like this, she had to be out on a somewhat-date with her ex in Chestnut Ridge. If she was alone in her apartment, she wouldn't have to face anyone, but here it was different.

The front door screeched open behind her. "Everything okay out here?" Chase stood in the doorway, seeming genuinely concerned.

She wiped the few tears from her eyes, hoping her mascara didn't smear. "No, everything is not okay. Nothing is okay. I need you to take me home."

"But we . . . " he stopped mid-sentence.

"Chase," she said sternly, turning so he could see her face. "I want to go home. Now. Can you get your keys and not make me explain every little detail to you please?"

"Sure thing," he said. He mumbled something under his breath as he disappeared back into the house. Arriving minutes later with her jacket, he swung it over her shoulders and they strode to the car, avoiding eye contact.

Though the ride was short, the dead air between them made it awkward, very much in contrast to the lighthearted ride over. Chase tapped his fingers on the steering wheel and messed with the heat to fill the time, occasionally stealing a look in her direction.

"I gotta ask. You seem really upset. Is everything ok?" He waited briefly for an answer before continuing. "Everything seemed to be going so well tonight. I thought you might actually be having fun."

"I'm fine," Tessa huffed. She didn't want to discuss her major failure with the boyfriend she'd left behind.

"Are you sure? You seemed to be enjoying yourself—we were dancing and then you ran outside, and now . . ."

"And now what, Chase?" she said through her teeth.

He turned toward her and motioned in her direction. "You're crying and clearly upset and I just don't want it to be because of me. I was having a great time with you. When we're together, it feels like you never left. But if being with me is upsetting you . . ."

Tessa slapped her leg in frustration. "And why would I be upset about you, Chase? We share one stupid dance to a Christmas song at a lame Chestnut Ridge party, and now I'm madly in love with you again?" Chase's eyes filled with both shock and hurt. "It has nothing to do with you. It never had anything to do with you."

Chase cleared his throat. "I didn't say you were madly in love with me."

Tessa snapped back at him, raising her voice to a high school-level fight. "Well I'm not, Chase. If I was, I would have returned your calls all those years ago. I didn't want Chestnut Ridge then, and I didn't want you, and now I'm back here for two lousy weeks and everything falls apart in my life at home. My job is ruined—who knows if I even have one to go back to—and I'm stuck here doing the exact things I never wanted to do. Play house with you at a party full of people who got married young and sent their kids to the babysitter so they could dress up in stupid costumes."

Chase looked visibly stung, and Tessa felt she had gone too far. Though they both knew some of it was true, never had she been so blatantly honest with him before. Even her e-mail breaking up with him was intentionally vague—she'd never wanted to spell it out to him so clearly. Chase swatted a tear from his eye and reached for the radio dial, turning the volume tolerably high, and quickly switching from the festive tunes to a classic rock station.

A word wasn't said between them the rest of the ride home. When he pulled in her driveway, she reached on the floor to grab her purse and stopped before getting out. She looked over at him, his jaw tight as he looked dead ahead. "I'm sorry, Chase. I shouldn't have yelled at you. I just got really bad news while we were at the party and I'm upset about that."

Chase stared ahead and clicked the button on the armrest to unlock the door. Exhaling, she pulled the handle and stood from the car. She looked down at Chase and considered saying more, like she hadn't meant what she said—it was always about him—but slammed the door instead. Before she could even walk around the car and head toward the door, he reversed the car to the end of the driveway and pulled away, the tires spinning the slush up from the pavement as he drove off. He was clearly angry, and she couldn't blame him after the way she'd just treated him.

"Ugh!" Tessa kicked at the snow, slipping a bit before catching herself, her legs sliding apart. "I hate it here!" She said out loud, though there was no one to hear her. "I hate Chestnut Ridge!"

Chapter 13

Stomping up the steps to the door, she let herself in with her key and walked straight to the counter to the open bottle of wine, pulling a glass from the cabinet. She sat at the kitchen table and scrolled through e-mails on her phone, reading some of the exchange between Ben and Jay. She grew increasingly more angry with herself for listening to Ben and completely disconnecting this past week. If she had followed along, there might have been something she could've said, but instead she was pushed out completely. How could she have been so foolish to take his advice and leave town when the firm was planning such an important meeting? Normally she would have insisted on having more control. Why did she give in so easily? And who knew where she stood with the company now.

Most of the other large accounts at the firm had lead directors already assigned to them. Jay's was the biggest account and had been her baby since she was an assistant on it at twenty-two. Managing Jay's provided the coveted seniority over others in the office, even those who had been with the firm longer. This account had been a major step up the ladder to her success.

Of course Ben would swoop in last minute, having put zero work into the account, and save the day. Advertising was a cutthroat industry, and he knew how to play it to his advantage better than anyone else.

Tessa opened her messages and went back to the open string with Ben.

Keep me in the loop. I know Jay better than anyone. We can fix this.

She sat, grudgingly sipping her wine and looking to her phone for a reply that never came. As she watched for new incoming messages, she looked at Chase's name, his cheery note from earlier visible at the top of their conversation. It wasn't his fault that this happened tonight, and it also wasn't his fault she messed up at work and was back in Chestnut Ridge. Nothing had ever been his fault, and he certainly didn't deserve her yelling at him the way she did. Opening their conversation, she typed, *I had a great time tonight. I'm so sorry.* She added a sad face, but as she looked down at the phone, she decided to quickly delete it before she sent it by accident. She then typed a simple *I'm sorry* but again decided to erase it.

Her mom, wrapped in a plush winter robe, appeared in the doorway.

"You're home early. Did you have fun at the party?" She rubbed her eyes awake after having dozed off.

"I don't want to talk about it. I should never have come back here. Everything I've worked so hard for is ruined now because of this place . . . everything. I'll probably be stuck here for the rest of my sad life, living here with you." Tessa plopped her forehead down on her crossed arms on the table.

"Whoa, Tessa. Calm down, sweetie. Did something happen at the party?"

Lifting her head, she said, "No, Mom, nothing happened at the party. Nothing ever happens in Chestnut Ridge, that's the point. Everyone here just lives in their tiny little bubble and does their tiny little things. It's pathetic! You should have seen all these people at the party, talking to the same people about the same things. It couldn't have been more depressing."

It wasn't entirely the truth—she'd been having a decent time at the party before she heard from Ben. Ashley and Zak couldn't have been nicer, and Jana looked like she might have welcomed a conversation if Tessa had stayed a little longer. And then there was Chase. She couldn't recall the last time she'd had that much fun. But after the bomb Ben dropped on her, the small-town world of Chestnut Ridge didn't seem to matter. Eventually her two-week visit would be up and she'd have to return to her life, and based on what she heard today, it could be drastically different. Even if Jay stayed on, she'd have a lot to prove.

Her mom groaned and rolled her eyes. "I'm tired of listening to this, Tessa. Seriously, so tired of it. You turn your nose up to this place and all of us like we're some sort of second-class citizens living a second-class life. I happen to *like* Chestnut Ridge, and I would imagine that the rest of the people who live here feel the same way. I think it's peaceful—I like the feeling I get when I go to the market and see familiar faces. I like the things the community does for one another. It doesn't have to be what you want for your life, but just because it's not what you want, doesn't make it not good enough for someone else. Maybe Chestnut Ridge is exactly what the people who live here want, and maybe your choices look silly to them."

Tessa, preoccupied with her phone, just shook her head. Her phone remained clear—no messages from Ben or Chase, though she didn't expect Chase to contact her first.

Her mom was clearly frustrated now. "You don't have anything to say to that?"

"No, I don't. I don't know how anyone could like it here."

Shaking her head, her mom turned to go back upstairs. "Well, that's just sad, Tessa. Because I like it here, and your nana loved it. We gave you a good life in Chestnut Ridge and all you ever did was act like you couldn't get away from us fast enough."

"That's not true. Nana was always telling me to dream big, experience things. Don't be afraid to live to the fullest. She never wanted me to stay here and end up doing the same thing as everyone else."

"That's very true, Tess. She lived her own life that way too. If she ended up here and stayed here, don't you think she realized her life was fullest right where she was?"

Taking another glance at her phone before looking back her mom, she said, "I'm sorry. I'm not trying to fight or hurt your feelings. My boss called with some upsetting news about work, and I don't know if it's something I can fix."

Her mom walked down the hall and started up the steps. "It's a little too late for that, honey. I'll see you in the morning."

Slamming her phone onto the kitchen table, she put her head in her hands, her temples pulsing from the stress. Not only did she get horrible news from work, but Chase was furious with her—rightfully so—and now she'd hurt her mom too. Everything in her life seemed to have fallen apart in just a few short hours. So much for Christmas magic. The closer she got to the holiday, the worse off she got.

Across the table, her nana's cookbook sat open to a recipe her mom had picked out for the next day. She stood up and leaned across the table, grabbing the corner of the book to slide it back toward her. "Ugh. Nana"—she flipped through the pages—"I could sure use a hot cocoa right now."

Though Nana would have listened to her, she would not have been happy that Tessa upset her mom. That was her one rule, no matter what, and Tessa had always known it. Nana was Mom's biggest advocate and cheerleader, constantly bragging about how hard she worked to provide for them all. Her mom had worked an office job and sometimes picked up odd jobs at night too. Her nana never missed an opportunity to remind Tessa to be grateful for her mom's selfless work ethic. "She never wanted you to feel like you had to want for anything," she'd say. "That's hard enough for two parents to accomplish for their children—imagine the responsibility with just one. And she does it all with a smile." And it was the truth, her mom did. She'd never complained about her situation, even though she never put herself first and provided a charmed childhood for Tessa.

As she turned the pages of the recipe book, a thought came to mind. Maybe through cooking the recipes, and experiencing the flavors from Tessa's childhood, her mom was trying to relive the days when they were closer and happier as a family. Each recipe they recreated from the book was served with a heaping side of memories from their past. Most of them delightfully as bright as the taste of the food. Tessa had been so busy trying to make something of her own life that she hadn't stopped to see how lonely her mom might be. With her only daughter living in New York and Nana gone, she was all alone here. Living in the same house, the same life where the memories she cherished were made.

Tessa stopped on one of her favorite recipes that Nana made each year for Christmas Eve as part of her traditional Italian Feast of the Seven Fishes, her homemade Clams Oreganata. Nana new that Tessa loved seafood, and she would often make upwards of nine or ten different dishes for Christmas Eve—far past the traditional seven that was part of the tradition. As she turned to the next page, she noticed a piece of folded paper that had been tucked in the crease of the book. Tessa recognized the stationary as her nana's, one of the many free floral pads she'd received as a thank you from donating to various charities. This distinct stationary was Nana's favorite because of its pink color and cherry blossom border. She would use it sparingly, choosing a sheet of paper from one of her many other pads if it was just for a simple task or list. She saved the pink paper for what she deemed more important matters—notes to friends that she'd send through snail mail or anything she had to write up for the church.

Across the front of the fold, she saw her name. "Tessy," with a large, swirling *y* like her nana used to write on her birthday cards, and a heart for a period following her name. She picked up the paper with both hands and stared at it before tearing off the snowflake sticker that was holding it closed, and she opened the letter.

The note was a few paragraphs long, scripted in her nana's unsteady handwriting.

My Petunia,

I'm hoping by leaving this on one of your favorite recipes, that you will find it. And not because you are rifling through aimlessly, but because you have taken up cooking some of the recipes we used to make together. When we started this book, you were such a fiery young thing, curious about everything. You asked me to share with you all my secrets in the kitchen so you could cook delicious meals for your family one day, as I did for you.

I've never been able to put into words the amount of joy it has brought me to cook together, or how much fun I've had watching you learn, and that of all the people in your life, you chose to look up to me. I so much wanted to show you that you could be anything you dreamed of in the world, and like many people, I didn't want you to be afraid to go out there and get it. You were always the brightest bulb on the string of lights, and I wanted you to believe just how special you are.

But over these past few years I've watched you lose your spirit. I can hear it when you call, that you are taking your life too seriously and forgetting to stop and smell the cooking. I'm fearful that you've forgotten what's important and what truly matters most. I get to say this because I'm an old lady (no, I will never admit this to you again, but I am old), and the best piece of advice I could give you is that this beautiful life goes fast, Tessy. There are so many magical moments that can't be bought, and there are many life achievements that are filled with much more meaning than a promotion at work.

Try not to miss out on all the magnificent moments because you're stuck up there in that office. There's no job that is worth your happiness. I want you to look at the world the way your tiny round eyes would look at our Christmas Eve feast, like

there were so many delightful options and you didn't know where

to start. And you never had to choose just one. Fall in love, eat

the extra piece of cheese, have a glass of wine at noon just

because. Most of all, remember to stop and smell the cooking.

Otherwise, when you finally realize what you missed out on along

the way, it might be too late. There's never just one path in life, it

should be full of many. I love you, Tessy, my petunia.

Nana

Tessa barely noticed the tears gathering in her eyes. Was it that obvious to Nana that she'd been working too hard and focusing on the wrong things? And why hadn't Nana tried to talk to her about this in person, when she was still here. She could have tried. She remembered times over the phone when Nana would tell her to slow down or to call out sick—spend the day in bed eating ice cream. Of course, Tessa never listened. She'd brush off her recommendations and remain focused on her work. She was always thinking about the next campaign, the next client dinner, the next promotion.

Hoping for more from Nana, she turned the page over to the next recipe. It was Nana's homemade calamari recipe with a sticky note that read, "Mom's favorite, but she'll never make it." Tessa wiped her eyes and chuckled. Nana might not be here, but she was still running the show, and for the first time Tessa was going to slow down and listen.

Nana's homemade calamari was legendary, specifically because it was a difficult recipe to make just right. Like her mom, most people either bought the fish frozen—some even buying it pre-breaded—or opted to purchase it from a restaurant to save the trouble. But Nana would start the recipe from scratch, slicing the fresh fish and frying it to perfection. Her secret brine and breading cooked for just the right amount of time delivered a mouthwatering bite-sized ring. After being tossed in a squeeze of lemon juice and sprinkled with parsley, she'd serve it with her homemade tomato sauce. It was better than any of the restaurants in town and one of the first dishes to disappear each Christmas Eve. All the guests would wait by the table for it to be served, knowing Nana only made it once a year. Her mom loved it and would beg Nana to make it for other occasions, but she'd wave her hands and tell her, "absolutely no." Which only made the dish even more special.

Tessa watched her nana make it many times but never helped—she was always shooed out of the way and assigned to another task. Nana took pride in all her recipes, but her homemade calamari was at the top of her list. She couldn't risk Tessa slicing the rings too thin or overcooking it. She made it carefully and with love every time.

The Christmas Eve feast presented the perfect opportunity to make things up to her mom. Paging through the following recipes, she quickly made a mental list of the seafood dishes she would suggest that they prepare. It was an unwritten family law that the feast started with homemade pizza and that there was always a pasta dish to accompany the seafood. Looking over the recipes, she decided to cut back from the ten fish choices Nana would've made and stick with the traditional seven, deciding it was better to have seven well-prepared dishes than to overextend herself and try to make more.

Feeling rejuvenated, Tessa picked up her phone and quickly typed out a message to Chase. *I'm so sorry for how I acted tonight. You didn't deserve it. Forgive me?*

She didn't know if he'd answer, but apologizing seemed like a good place start. Turning her attention back to the recipe book, Tessa fanned through the pages until she saw her nana's homemade Italian bread recipe. Nana used to make it once a week for her mom—it was high on the list of her favorites—but since Nana made it more, it was easy to take advantage of. Reading over the instructions, she saw that she'd have to let the bread rise for at least an hour. With a quick glance at the clock on the stove, she saw it was close to midnight. She'd pulled later nights, so she reached up to get a mixing bowl from the cabinet and began to search for the ingredients, hoping her mom had all that she needed. It wouldn't be the first time she'd stayed up late—all-nighters were in her job description—and making it up to her mom was much more important than a client presentation.

Over two hours later, it was near three in the morning, and the utensils and bowls were washed and put away as she waited on the last few minutes of the baking. The smell of the freshly-baked bread wafted through the house, bringing with it a homey feeling. When the timer buzzed, she carefully opened the oven door and pulled out a perfect, golden-brown loaf. More than pleased with the result, she allowed the bread to cool on a rack while she wrote a note to her mom.

Sorry for hurting your feelings last night. Maybe some fresh-baked bread will help?

I love you.

Tessa

After covering the bread so it would stay soft, she glanced over the kitchen one last time to make sure the oven was off and everything was cleaned. Taking in a whiff of her bread, she smiled before switching off the light, silently promising Nana that her message was well received.

Chapter 14

Early the next morning, her eyelids slow to open from the combination of wine and late-night bread making, she splashed water on her face before hurrying down the stairs. She slowed at the end of the hall and saw her mom at the table, a thick-cut slice of her bread smeared with butter and fig jam, sitting on a plate in front of her. Her mom seemed more than content as she leafed through the Sunday newspaper.

"I see you found my peace offering. I'm sorry, Mom." After reading Nana's letter, she felt awful for how she treated her mother.

Her mom looked up. "So that's what this is? An olive branch? Think you can buy my love with carbs, huh?"

Smiling, Tessa walked over and placed two hands on her mom's shoulders, leaning over with a knowing look. Her mom loved carbs more than anything—chocolate, wine—she'd pick a solid slice of bread any day.

"Everyone knows I'm a sucker for homemade bread, especially heavenly bread like this," her mom said as she snuck a quick kiss on Tessa's hand. Her face shone from her mother's compliment.

Happy to see that her mom appeared to be letting her off easy, she filled her coffee mug and went to slice a piece of bread for herself. "Thanks for forgiving me. I knew you'd like the bread, but I thought you still might be mad at me."

"Hey, hey, hey!" her mom said, teasingly taking the knife from her hand. "You're gonna have to work a little harder if you expect me to share with you."

"I said I'm sorry," she pleaded with a smile, reaching behind her mother's back for the bread knife.

"And . . . ?" Her mom held the knife farther away from her.

"And what? You're not going to make me say I like being in Chestnut Ridge, are you? Cause that may be pushing your luck."

"No, I won't make you say you like it, but I am going to make you tell me how wonderful of a job I did raising you here."

"Seriously, Mom, you need me to actually say it?"

"Absolutely . . . And I don't have all day. You told Mr. Flatts you'd go early to the tree lighting tonight to help, and I still have to make the penne."

Tessa had forgotten all about the pageant and tree lighting tonight, and that she had promised Mr. Flatts she'd help set up the potluck. "I forgot that was tonight."

"I'm waiting, Tessy." Her mom mockingly tapped her slipper against the tile.

Tessa tilted her head forward, one last attempt to stop the joke, before caving. "Fine! I had a wonderful childhood here in Chestnut Ridge, and it was all because of you, Mom. You're the best."

Twirling the butter knife in front of her before pointing it at Tessa, she said, "That's right, missy, and don't you ever forget that." Thrilled with her victory, her mom handed over the knife. Tessa snatched it before slicing through the perfectly-textured loaf and slathering it with butter, taking a huge bite.

Between chews, she said, "Wow, I did pretty darn good, didn't I? Tastes close to Nana's."

She considered whether to tell her mom about the letter she found in the recipe book, and decided to hold back. When asked what made her have a change of heart and decide to bake bread in the middle of the night, she shrugged and said she knew she was wrong. For reasons unknown, the letter seemed private. It was something she could keep between just her and Nana, and she didn't want to take away from how special that was. For now, she was grateful her mom had forgiven her for her outburst. Based on the lack of activity coming from her phone, Chase wasn't going to give in as easily.

***

One large pot of homemade vodka sauce and three boxes of penne later, they were on their way down to the town center to help Mr. Flatts set up the finishing touches on the potluck dinner to take place that night. After dropping one tray in a chafing dish at the buffet and bringing the remaining three back to the kitchen to be reheated as needed, Tessa walked back out to the courtyard to see where else she could lend a hand. She saw quite a few familiar faces stringing up lights. Many that she recognized as friends of either her mom or Nana. She nodded and waved at welcoming smiles as she passed each volunteer, looking for Mr. Flatts. When she found him out back rummaging through the storage shed, far from the courtyard to where the lawn stretched, she quickly rushed over to help him.

"Looking for something particular?" she asked, after knocking twice on the exterior doorframe so he wouldn't startle. He was clearly caught up in his search.

"Tessa, dear! Thanks for coming." Despite the cold temperatures his face was shining from sweat.

Bending over to move a box out of the way for him, she said, "I'm happy to help and, as you know, this was one of Nana's favorite events of the year. She'd start looking forward to it as soon as summer ended. It feels right to be a part of it."

"Speaking of your nana," he said, turning back to the piles of town-owned Christmas decorations. "I'm looking for the angel that she made for the top of the tree. I know it's in here somewhere, it's just gotta be. But I can't seem to find it anywhere among all this junk."

Tessa went down to one knee and began searching through the open boxes and containers on the opposite side from where Mr. Flatts was looking. Nana made the angel for the town when Tessa was in middle school. She was surprised that it was still being used to top the tree. Nana had sewn on a dazzling gold dress to replace the plain white frock that the angel had come in when she purchased it from the big box store to donate to the town. Back then, they'd collect decorations each year to use for the various events, but based on the boxes piled high in the shed, it appeared the town now had plenty to choose from. When they chose the angel in the store, Nana said she loved the face, but everything else could use an upgrade. So she sewed a new dress and even replaced the puny, wired wings with more elaborate ones, complete with a crystal trim and rhinestones lined throughout. When they'd catch the light from the strings that circled the tree below, they'd sparkle like a five-carat diamond ring, sending bits of light cascading around and giving off the impression that it was flying. Each year, after the children performed the pageant, when they'd begin the tree lighting ceremony, the town would countdown and she'd anxiously wait to see her angel lit in the sky. When the tree was finally plugged in, Nana's eyes lit up at the sight of her angel. Sitting up top, looking down over the town in her exquisite handmade attire.

"I can't break my promise to her. Long ago, I told her that as long as I'm running the tree lighting, I'll make sure her angel is the one sitting perched on top of the town tree." He looked concerned as he searched around the shed. "And now I can't find the darn thing."

Tessa reached for a box that was partly sticking out from under the shelving and pulled it out by its open flaps. "I'm sure we'll find it. It has to be in here somewhere—it's not like it could've walked off."

"You would hope not. I'd hate to see such a beautiful tradition end because a volunteer doesn't know the right spot to put something back. All the decorations go in this shed. It's not hard—you pack them up and put them away."

"I'm sure it's here in the shed, Mr. Flatts." Tessa tried to reassure him. She watched his hunched back and rickety knees as he sifted through the boxes, and it seemed he might be overextending himself. "Why don't you let me look for it, that way you can go get started on something else. Nana would hate it even more if her potluck wasn't just right because we were both in here digging around for her angel. Not to mention it's freezing out here!"

With a labored breath, Mr. Flatts agreed. He struggled to stand straight, so Tessa stood and reached for his arm so he could balance himself. "I never want to admit it, but this stuff gets harder and harder to run each year. Not that I don't want to do it still, but this old body just doesn't work like it used to."

"Nana used to say if you stop using it, you'll lose it. I think she would've walked to her own funeral if it was possible." Nana was fiercely headstrong and did everything she could for herself.

"Heck, I'm surprised she didn't," he said, looking off into the distance. "You promise you'll find the angel?"

Tessa nodded and stayed by Mr. Flatts' side as he stepped down the few boards to get down in the front of the shed. "I promise."

He placed his free hand on Tessa's arm, patting it gently. "You know, your nana talked about you almost every day. She was so proud of you and the woman that you grew up to be. A day didn't pass that she didn't have something to brag about her little petunia."

Tessa's cheeks lifted into a smile. "Thank you, that's so kind of you to say. Hopefully she didn't brag too much, though. You know she could be quite the talker."

"No, no, never. She thought it was great that you were doing your own thing." He rubbed her arm before letting go. "But she worried about you too. Thought you were working too hard, missing out on the fun stuff. She'd be so happy to see you here, volunteering in the community."

Nana had told her often over the phone that she worked too hard. "You two were close, huh?"

Mr. Flatts nodded his head in agreement. "Great friends. It's good to have an ally who's your age when you're an old bird like me. I used to go over to your house for lunch a few days a week. I loved her chicken pot pie. She'd always have it ready for me no matter how many times I stopped in. It's like she knew I was coming."

"That sounds like Nana. I swear she must've had special powers."

"I think she'd be thrilled you're back in town for a bit, helping out the town on one of her favorite nights. I bet she's up there giddy as can be right now."

Tessa's smile faded slightly. "I like to think that she'd be happy I'm here too."

Mr. Flatts tipped the corner of his newsboy cap and said, "I know she would be. Let me know when you find that angel. Deal? We gotta get her connected to the lights before the pageant."

Tessa said that she would, turned, and bent back over the boxes, digging through each one before moving it to the side to start on the next. Twenty minutes later, she had made it through half of the boxes in the shed and still hadn't found the angel. She sat back against one of the boxes to catch her breath when she saw a shoebox she recognized, pushed to the back corner of the shed, and tucked under some spare shelving. She crawled across the worn wood floor and reached her arm as far as she could under the shelf. When she still couldn't reach it, she grabbed a snow shovel that was propped up against the wall and gently swatted at the box, pushing it forward, and bringing with it a cloud of dirt and dust.

Coughing away the tiny bits that got kicked up as high as her mouth, Tessa turned her head away, picked up the box, and wiped the top off with her forearm before opening it. Inside, laid out on a soft bedding of folded linen napkins, was her nana's angel. The dress and enchanting wings were just as beautiful as she remembered them. Tracing the beads on the outline of each wing with her finger, Tessa could remember watching in awe as her nana stitched the crystals around the edges. She held the angel up in front of her and examined the dress, brushing it flat before delicately placing it back into the shoebox and replacing the lid.

She brought it to Mr. Flatts, and his face burst from within as he too traced the angel's intricate features with his thumb.

"Would you do the honor tonight of placing her on the tree?" he said without lifting his eyes to meet hers.

"Are you sure there's no one better for the job? I don't even live here year-round. I wouldn't want anyone to be offended that I'm the one doing it." She also wanted to avoid being the center of the town's attention.

"Offended? You grew up here. You're Chestnut Ridge through and through. Plus, your nana would want it this way. She was proud to welcome back all to Chestnut Ridge." Nana did keep tabs on who left and who returned, always sure to drop off a neighborly plate of cookies to welcome them back to town.

Tessa took the box from his hands and stared back at the angel. "I'd be honored then. But how do I get all the way up there? That's a tall tree."

Brushing it off as if it was nothing, Mr. Flatts said, "With a ladder, of course. Don't worry, we'll get you all set up and show you what to do." Before she could object, he scooted past her to instruct some of the other volunteers who were decorating around the tree and adding the finishing touches to the Nativity scene where the kids would put on their pageant. He turned over his shoulder, yelling in her direction that they needed more straw for the manger as he pointed back toward the shed she'd just come from. She remembered seeing where the box of straw was stored. She turned to retrieve it, raising a single thumb above her head so he'd know she was on it.

More of the town began to file in as she returned with the straw. Mr. Flatts pressed it into the manger. The Nativity scene was set, and the children started to arrive with their parents, dressed as different characters or animals from the story of Christmas. They began gathering near the front of the courtyard waiting to be told to take their places to start, each fidgeting with their costumes. As she approached the group, she could see Ashley and Jana approaching, kids in tow, nitpicking at their hair, making last-minute adjustments, and pushing off their hands from messing too much with what they were wearing. She handed the remaining pieces of straw to Mr. Flatts before tapping Ashley on the shoulder, pulling her attention from her kids.

Seeming frazzled, Ashley picked at a string from her son's shoulder before she nudged him off to talk to his friends. "Tessa, hi!" she said as she watched him meet with the other kids. "What happened to you the other night? One minute we were all dancing and then, next thing I know, I look around and you guys were gone. I felt like a horrible host, I didn't even get to say goodbye."

Tessa understood that Ashley was implying more that she was a horrible guest for leaving unannounced, and without thanking her for the invitation. "I'm sorry I had to run off like that and drag Chase with me. I got a phone call from work that I had to address. It was time-sensitive and he was my ride."

On cue and seeming to already know the full story, likely from Chase, Ashley and Jana responded with "Oh" and "*Mm-hmm*" in unison. It was a subpar attempt at acting like it was the first they'd heard of it.

"Thank you for inviting me. I had a lovely time and wish I'd gotten to stay longer. It was a lot of fun." Tessa's mind turned to what might've happened if they'd stayed longer at the party.

"It was my pleasure," Ashley interrupted, noticeably less enthusiastic toward their friendship today than she was at the party. Either the martinis had worn off, or Chase already filled Zac in on how she acted toward him after they left. She assumed it had more to do with the latter.

Tessa nodded and turned to walk away before she stopped and spun back, Ashley and Jana each looking up in her direction.

"Jana, I could use some help organizing the food in the kitchen for the potluck. Can I pull you away for a second?"

Jana looked at Tessa, then to Ashley, then back, pulling her stare in and wrinkling her nose before grudgingly agreeing to help.

"Thank you," Tessa said, motioning her to lead the way. Jana walked, noticeably annoyed, to the kitchen, turning back once to roll her eyes at Ashley and unfazed that Tessa could also see.

Once inside the kitchen, Jana fumbled with a stack of paper plates, unwrapping the plastic holding the pack together and avoiding both eye contact and conversation.

Tessa cleared her throat, once with no reaction, before starting again. "I just wanted to say that I'm sorry. I know that I'm the reason we lost touch during college. It was a terrible thing for me to do. I completely fell off the face of the earth and stopped returning your calls, and that was selfish of me." Jana kept her eyes on the plates. "I never meant to hurt you—I just wanted to put as much distance between myself and this place as possible, and I guess I felt like I had to cut off everyone to do that. I'm not saying it was right, I'm just simply saying that's how I felt at the time, and I'm sorry."

Jana paused from fiddling with the paper products and looked up at Tessa. "That's all great, and Chase might accept your little apology and poor me pleas, but we were best friends for way longer than you two were together. Don't you think I needed my best friend through college? I wasn't just some guy you dated. We were friends for most of our lives, and you dropped me for no other reason than you felt that where you were from was beneath you. It did hurt, Tessa. It really did." Jana raised her hand to silence Tessa's response. "Imagine being in a new school, in a new town and not having that many friends yet, and your *best friend* that you've always counted on stops speaking to you. With no explanation, no reason. I was lonely Tessa, and I could've had you to talk to about that, but you were too busy mapping out your future and writing me and every other person who loved you out of it."

Tessa waited to speak up to see if Jana had more to say. "I didn't mean for it to happen that way. I was younger, naïve, not thinking about things long term. I just wanted to do what was right for me and I ended up hurting everyone else." Tessa leaned over the counter and reached for Jana's hand, trying to make her understand that she really was sorry.

"How is throwing away every relationship that you ever had the right thing to do? Me, Chase, your mom? What did any of us ever do to you that you felt the need to run away?" It was a question she didn't have an answer to.

"It's nothing you or my mom or Chase did. It's here, this place. Chestnut Ridge can be so suffocating, and you know how badly I wanted to get out of here. I know that more than anyone, you understood that. You always said you felt the same way."

Jana shook her head. "That's where you're wrong, Tess. I only said that to agree with you back then. I never felt those things. Sure, it might have been cool to leave Chestnut Ridge and try something new, but my family is here. My friends . . . my husband now. I'm proud of my life here. The sad thing is, you're the only one who isn't. And none of us deserve that from you."

Tessa opened her mouth but couldn't find the words to defend herself. Jana was right—none of them did deserve it. With little explanation, she left them and didn't return. Even Nana seemed to feel like she'd abandoned her roots to try to build a better life.

"All I can say is that I'm sorry. And you don't have to forgive me, but I want you to know that I understand what I did to you was wrong. We don't have to be best friends again—I'm not expecting anything like that. I just wanted you to know that it wasn't you. It was me, and I'm sorry."

With a tightlipped smile, Jana thanked Tessa before asking if she actually needed help in the kitchen or if she only asked her to talk. Tessa said she was fine finishing up without her and that she could go back out to where they were setting up for the pageant. "My boys are probably seconds away from knocking down the Christmas tree. I can't leave them alone for two seconds without one of them breaking something." Tessa laughed. Before, it had been hard to picture Jana as a mother, but seeing it now, it was clear she was a great one.

Once alone in the kitchen, she let the breath she was holding escape in an exasperated sigh. She hadn't expected Jana to have anything to say to her in return, but it would have been nice to hear that it wasn't all her fault. That wouldn't have been the truth, though. Part of her had hoped that Jana would say she forgave her, pulling her in for a long-overdue hug and laughing about how crazy it was that it had been so long since they last saw each other. Maybe everything could've gone back to how it was when they were close. But that didn't happen, and she was going to have to live with that for now. Soon enough, she'd be back in New York without daily reminders of the poor decisions she made in the past. There were many times in the city when she missed Jana's friendship, and she thought about Chase more times than that. But it was nothing like the persistent déjà vu she was experiencing being home. Everything about Chestnut Ridge reminded her of what was, for better or worse.

But unlike her job, Chestnut Ridge seemed open to accepting her back, despite her wrongdoings and hurtful decisions. Ben turned on her the first chance he got, disregarding years of dedication and hard work to save himself and making her sacrifice feel less and less worth it. His suggestion of a vacation did not come from a place of concern for her well-being, but a concern that she wouldn't be able to produce at the pace she had been for years. It was becoming clear that Ben didn't care about her, or how she felt about Christmas, for that matter. He cared about what she could do for him and the firm.

Alone in the kitchen, she began to wonder if any of it had been worth it. If she'd made different choices, would she and Chase be as in love and happy as Ashley and Zak? In the same kind of cutesy relationship reserved for starry-eyed teens? There was a chance her mom was right when she said some people chose a community like Chestnut Ridge. As she watched her old friends and family live their lives in this town, they seemed to have something she could never claim—they were relaxed and comfortable, merrily enjoying themselves and the lives they had.

Did her work make her happy, or did her dedication to her job stem from a need to prove herself? Even Chase, who'd had every reason to be mad with her, was willing to welcome her back into his life with open arms and start fresh at what could've been. If she'd never gotten that text from Ben, pulling her back to who she was, they would have danced all night, getting closer with each song. Nothing in New York stole her heart like Chase. The night of the party, decked out in her hideous sweater and surrounded by lost friends, she felt like she was floating on a cotton candy cloud, enjoying the night with ease in his company. When he held her hand, like they were a couple, she was reminded of how good it felt to be with someone who knows you better than you know yourself.

What she told Jana was true—back then, she was young and didn't understand the magnitude of her decisions. But she was older now and beginning to understand that the ones who are worth fighting for are the ones who would fight the same for you. Chase proved he'd always have her back, and Ben, her closest confidant in New York, abandoned her when his back was up against a wall. If there was one thing she'd learned from Nana, it was that if there was a will, there was a way. Nana never stopped making those around her feel special, and it was time for

her to do the same.

Chapter 15

Later that night, seated next to her mom, Tessa watched as the children from the town performed the same pageant she and her classmates had years earlier as kids themselves. The nerves of the children were familiar as they acted out their scenes in front of everyone they knew. She smiled when one young boy forgot his only line, leaving him sulking at the back of the nativity. She joined the rest of the crowd tittering under their breath as the girl chosen to be Mary pulled her robe out from under a boy who was stepping on it, sending him back on his bottom, feet in the air. The innocence of the children performing the story of Christmas was palpable—they excitedly bowed over and over, holding hands with one another at the end of the show before running to their parents' arms, ready to move on to the next part of the night.

As most gathered to congratulate their children on a job well done, Tessa shifted the contents of the potluck buffet, putting out last-minute items such as parmesan cheese near the pasta, and oil and vinegar near the salad. Her mom busied herself with stirring each of the dishes, making sure everything looked just right before she nodded to Mr. Flatts that the food was ready to be served. With one last look over her setup, she was satisfied that it looked as close to Nana's as it could without her being the one to do it herself.

The town filed into the room, forming a single line that snaked throughout. Looking over the crowd, Tessa felt a beaming sense of pride for her part in having helped organize the dinner, though it wasn't much. She knew her nana would feel the same. Toward the back of the line, in his standard flannel, she saw Chase. His eyes darted to the opposite side of the room when she noticed him looking her way.

Tessa's mom draped a single arm around her waist, tilting her head to whisper into her ear. "You two aren't avoiding each other, are you?"

"What makes you say that?" she asked, although she knew it was obvious.

"He couldn't have looked away fast enough. The other night, you two were staring at each other like two teenagers again. Something *did* happen at the party, didn't it?"

Facing her mom, one eye still on Chase, she said, "I was rude to him—actually, downright mean to him after I got the call from Ben." Her mom looked at her in the 'I'm your mom and know everything way' as Tessa continued. "Everything was going great, *really* great, but then I got that text and I was upset and didn't want anyone at the party to see me like that. I asked to go home, but he pushed and kept asking me if everything was ok. And I snapped. Yelled at him pretty hard. I tried to apologize to him that night, right after it happened, but he hasn't responded to me."

Her mom squeezed her waist. "We all make mistakes, honey. I'm sure he'll forgive you eventually." She raised her wrist to a slow wave in Chase's direction, which he returned before turning his attention back to Zac.

Tessa wasn't as sure he would forgive her this time. The way she saw it, Chase had already given her a second chance this week, and he didn't seem keen on giving her another. He could have left her stranded in the parking lot with Mr. Weaver, put his head down and acted like he didn't recognize her, but he chose to walk over and help her out. He made the first move by asking her to coffee, and then took the next step of inviting her to the party. Chase had tried to move on from what she did in their past, but she shattered all his efforts over a single text message about a client from work.

But things were moving so quickly at the party that night. She hadn't fully grasped what was happening. If Ashley hadn't interrupted them in the study, he might have kissed her, and she would have let him. If that had happened, where would they be? Standing in line together about to fix their plates? By nature, her heart called to him and craved to be with him, but she ended their relationship back then for a reason. She had a life in New York and he had his life here in Chestnut Ridge, and they couldn't be more opposite of each other. The north and south pole had more in common than her and Chase back then. He wanted small town and she needed the big city. Could she build a life here, as so many others had, in Chestnut Ridge?

As the line for the buffet died down, she noticed that Chase was no longer in it. She surveyed the room, looking for his mop of light-brown hair that always seemed to be flawlessly unkempt, but she didn't see it anywhere in the near vicinity. She considered looking for him outside, back where they'd had one of their first conversations together in years, but she opted to join the back of the line instead. She'd give him time to warm up to her over the course of the night. If she knew Chase like she thought she did, he wouldn't stay away for long.

When she got up to the string of tables filled with every type of food one could fathom, she scooped small portions of everything on her plate before sitting down in an empty chair next to her mom. Mr. Flatts complimented them both on how wonderful the flow was for the food and graciously thanked them for the help, repeating again that it was getting harder each year for him. She was casually listening as he told his story about how one year, they couldn't get enough people to donate to the dinner before Nana stepped in and made most of it herself. She thought she saw Chase come back into the room, so she stood and wiped her mouth, smiling wide and pointing at her teeth to her mom, who gestured she was ok. Taking one last sip of water, she excused herself before she walked over to where Chase was standing. When he saw her approaching, he looked around at first, like he might try to walk away before she reached him, but stood holding both his ground and his plate of food.

"Can I talk to you?" Tessa asked, skipping over a greeting and getting right to it.

"What's there to talk about? You made it clear how you feel about me the other night." He forked a scoop of pasta into his mouth.

"Don't do that, please—that thing where you pretend nothing is the matter, but it is. You know what I want to talk to you about, and I know you care what I have to say."

Sighing, he put his plate down on the table in front of him before forcefully rubbing his forehead. "You're right, Tess. Something is the matter. I was stupid enough to think that we maybe had another shot at this. I spent ten years getting over you, which I'm aware sounds ridiculous because it took you all of ten minutes to get over me, but it's the truth. And just when I thought things were going to be ok, and I could finally move on, you come waltzing back into my life. Then we're having a great time together, and I'm thinking that maybe you felt it too. But no."

Tessa reached for him, but he retracted his hands, tucking them in his front pockets and rocking back on his heels. "I told you what happened the other night. I told you that I got bad news from the office, and I was upset. It had nothing to do with you, and I shouldn't have lashed out."

"That's the thing," he said, looking around to see if his voice was getting too loud. "It's never about us or you even. It's always about your job, and I hate to tell you Tess, but that's all it is. A job. It's not who you are, it's what you do, and I feel bad for you that you put that above everything else in your life."

She tried to hide how bad his words stung. "That's not true . . . I'm trying to make things different."

"Yes, it is true. Look in the mirror. It's the only thing that matters to you. Not me, not your happiness, not your family. None of that is important enough to you, and I just can't keep sitting here allowing myself to be hurt by that. I'm sorry, Tess, but that's not fair to me."

She looked at him, wanting so badly to tell him that it wasn't the truth, but her words weren't there. Pulling his hand from his pocket, he wrapped it tightly around hers and squeezed. "I'll see you around, Tess."

Her heart sank as she watched him walk away, but she wouldn't allow herself to show it in front of all these people. She wanted to run after him, promise that she wanted things to be different, but instead she turned to make a dash for the ladies' room. Just as she was about to exit, Mr. Flatts announced that the tree lighting would begin in ten minutes. She stopped and took a deep breath to gather herself. Picking up her and her mom's coats from the rack, she walked back over to their table.

"How'd that go?" she asked, looking hopeful as Tessa said under her breath that she didn't want to talk about it.

Outside, the cold air turned her cheeks a bright pink. She stood off to the side of the crowd, wondering why the traditions were held outside when the temperature was typically close to freezing this time of year in Chestnut Ridge. People began to sing "O Christmas Tree" as the remaining guests filled in the back. The younger children ran to the front, bopping up and down, anxiously waiting for the tree to be lit.

Mr. Flatts stood at the front, both hands in the air hushing the crowd as they wrapped up the final verse of the song.

"Thank you all for coming! And a very special thank-you to all those who helped put on this wonderful evening. It takes a village, and the very best village, we have." The crowd clapped their hands, passing kind smiles to each other. "It's important to remember this time of year and all year long, how remarkable it is that we are such a tight-knit community here in Chestnut Ridge. I know that I have counted on many of you over the years to help me when I've needed it, and it brings me great joy that we live in a town where we can all count on each other. As we continue in this holiday season toward Christmas, I want all of you to remember that life is a beautiful thing. There are so many magical moments that make it what it is, and no matter how old we are, we should never forget that. Without further ado, drum roll, please!" The crowd patted their knees and clapped their hands as the eager smiles took over the childrens' faces, from their eyes to their chins.

Raising his arms in the air again, the drumming slowed. "This year we're welcoming back someone who grew up here in Chestnut Ridge, and who is the granddaughter of the very special lady who made our tree's angel. It only feels right that we let her top the tree. Tessa Gee, come on up!" Tessa, cheeks now punch red, walked to the front while the audience clapped their hands. Taking the angel from Mr. Flatts, she paused to look at it closely once more before climbing up the ladder, careful not to slip in front of the entire town. The tree was much bigger than it looked, and even though she was standing on the top run, she had to fully extend her arm and stand on the tips of her toes to place the angel on top. She fluffed the angel's dress over the top of the tree, taking one final look to make sure it was just so, then she turned back toward the crowd.

Mr. Flatts riled up the applause, then pointed to Zak who returned a two thumbs-up before plugging in the tree. The town cheered as the lights lit up the square, Nana's angel sitting up top, casting its twinkling light down on the audience. Tessa sighed at its beauty allowed a childish grin to creep over her face, taken aback by the moment of lighting the small town's tree.

All her years living in New York, she'd watched as people fought crowds to stand in awe under the tree in Rockefeller Center, and she never quite grasped the concept. But under this tree—her hometown tree that was decorated with love from so many—she understood. The feeling of Christmas in your community warms you from the inside out. Raising her hand to her lips, she motioned a kiss toward the angel, promising her nana that she understood now. She knew what she meant about enjoying all the tiny moments that make up your life.

Feeling someone's eyes on her as she climbed down the ladder, she looked across the crowded square. Chase was off to the side, staring back at her with a coy smirk, brushing his hair back from his eyes. She could see they were looking back at her sweetly, as if to say it wasn't over. Shaking his head with a laugh, he turned and made his way back over to his car, and deep down she could feel that she'd see him again.

With a new burst of energy, she rushed over to her mom who locked her arms around her. "Isn't the tree beautiful this year, Tessy? And the angel—every year I forget how magnificent it is."

"It really is," she said. "I have an idea that I might need your help with."

"Anything. What you thinking?"

"I want to make Christmas Eve dinner, like we said. But not just for me and you. I'd like to invite a few people over to join us if that's ok."

"Of course it is!" Her mom dropped one arm, but lifted the other to her shoulders as they walked toward the car. A different group of volunteers was responsible for cleaning up after the dinner. "Who are you thinking?"

Once secure in the car with the door shut, Tessa answered, "I want to invite Chase. I don't know what I'm thinking, but something just seems right this time with him. He hasn't forgiven me just yet, but I know that there's hope. I want to make it up to him with the best Christmas Eve ever."

"I think that's a great idea. And who could turn down our Christmas Eve feast? I remember him always hinting for an invitation back when you two were together." He spent Christmas Eve with her family during the years they dated.

"I'm hoping he won't be able to say no," Tessa said, an edge of worry to her tone.

Her mom placed a hand on her left knee. "You know all I ever wanted was for you to be happy. I never cared what you chose, as long as you were happy."

With a soft smile, Tessa said. "I know that, and I am happy . . . or I thought I was. But then I was forced on this leave, and ever since that last conversation with Ben—the one that ruined everything around here—I've just been thinking about things differently, I guess. The job doesn't care about me, but that's ok, because plenty of people here do."

"Forced leave? That's news to me."

Tessa placed a hand on her mom's. "I didn't want you to think it was the only reason I came home for Christmas. But I blew it in a meeting with our biggest client, Jay's Jewelers. I put together a last-minute holiday campaign for them, and they said it was uninspired. They told me I was cold. The client has been with us since the firm started, and they might be leaving now and it's my fault. That's the text I got the other night." She hoped her mom would understand the severity and why it had hit her so hard. "Regardless, after the meeting, Ben told me I was worn down, was focusing too much on work, and demanded that I take a break and use up my paid time off."

Her mom nodded, and Tessa could tell she was disappointed that her decision to take the time off was not made on her own. "Well, however it happened, you're here now. And this has been the best Christmas gift I ever could've been given."

"I've really enjoyed being here, and I'm not just saying that. Like tonight, when they lit the tree, I felt like a kid again, staring up at the lights. I think I felt the magic that I've been missing. I never thought I'd say it, but I feel like it's been good for me to come home to Chestnut Ridge. It's been good for me to be with you."

Her mom smiled, and in an exaggerated gesture, she flapped a hand in front of her eyes. "Don't make me tear up. My only daughter, my pride and joy, likes being with me."

She ignored her mom's jab. "Chase told me that I care more about what I do than who I am. Do you think he's right?"

After considering the thought, she said, "Honey, I think you can change what you think about your life and shift your priorities anytime you want. It was important for you to get out there, do things and see things. It was what you always wanted. You would have always regretted it, or wondered 'what if' if you hadn't experienced it for yourself. But it sounds like it's not really working for you anymore. Sure, you have the job and the clothes, the apartment with its glamorous zip code. But that can't take the place of family and a home. There's always a balance, and part of the fun in life is finding it."

Tessa thought about the idea of balance and tried to imagine where she saw herself in the next few years, but a clear picture didn't paint. "When I left, I didn't realize I hurt as many people as I did. I hope you know that. I didn't think anyone cared that much about me or the choices I was making." Honestly, she thought eventually everyone would move on and forget about her.

"Don't be silly. There're a lot of people that care for you. I'm your Mom—I love you no matter what you choose. Some others, you may have to try a little harder for," she said with a wink. "We'll make the best Christmas Eve dinner we've ever made. I don't know a man in the world that would turn that down."

Feeling confident after discussing the idea with her mom, she reached for her phone to invite Chase.

Christmas Eve dinner at my house? Please say yes.

She tossed her phone back into her purse and decided there was no need to wait for the response. She'd stay positive and look forward to her dinner. This time, she wouldn't be the one who stopped trying—she'd find a way to get him to come to dinner, and she'd make him believe that she'd heard what he said and that she wanted things to be different. Whether it be hope or the spirit of the season, she wanted to believe she had another chance.

"So, did your client really call you cold?" her mom asked, interrupting her thoughts.

Tessa let out a drawn-out sigh. "Actually, yes. In front of a room full of people."

Her mom burst into a fit of laughter as Tessa whined. "What's so funny about that? It was horrible!"

"I have to admit, that's pretty bad, Tess. Or should I say, Ms. Grinch."

"Hey, not fair! I just told you I'm working on it!" Tessa said, her mom having a fit over her comparison.

"So, what did you put in the presentation to get that reaction? Reindeer poop?" Her mom said, cracking herself up again.

Tessa told her the truth. "It's not what I put in, it's what I didn't. Apparently there wasn't enough feeling or emotion behind the concept. A jewelry store saying it's not all about gifts around Christmas . . . how ironic."

"I don't think it's ironic at all. Think about it, Tessy. A person only buys someone jewelry because they're looking for a gift that is as unique and special as that person. You don't buy just anyone jewelry—you buy it for a girlfriend, your wife, your mom. And you don't just pick anything out of the case—you look for the one beautiful piece that, when that special someone opens it, they'll know exactly what you're trying to say."

Tessa rolled her eyes and grunted. "I get it, I blew it. Everyone seems to get it right but me."

Her mom broke off into her own in-depth theory, and a thought came to mind. Each year, she'd sent her mom a package for Christmas that contained the standard gifts for women— scarves, kitchen items, perfume. But as she listened to her mom, her mind flashed back to that first day after her meeting with Jay when she'd walked into the store, searching for what she'd missed in her campaign. She remembered the woman and the request that she had for the saleswoman, for something special. Thinking back, she remembered the joy in the woman's eyes when she was told it was possible, and she realized that maybe her own mom would like something similar. Peeking down at her mom's hands on the steering wheel, she saw they were bare. Tessa knew her mom had Nana's wedding ring upstairs in her jewelry box, but she never saw her wear it on her own hand.

Realizing that Christmas was near and that she had little time, she typed "Jay's Jewelers" into the search bar on her phone to find the nearest store location. Coming from Chestnut Ridge, she'd have to drive at least a half hour to the closest shopping area, but she could make that work.

Sure, her mom always loved and appreciated anything that Tessa gave her, from the childhood noodle necklaces to the boxes of gifts she sent as an adult. But what if she could get her something truly special, something that she would always remember about this Christmas? She wanted her to know how much this time meant to her and now, she had the perfect idea for a gift. As her phone revealed the closest Jay's Jewelers, she realized she might be able to pull it off. Hopefully her mom kept Nana's ring in the same place she always had. She'd have to find a way to borrow it without her mom noticing.

She sat back in her seat and stared out the window, energized by her ideas to make it up to those who mattered the most to her. Her plans were in place. All she needed now was a bit of that Christmas magic others so faithfully believed in.

Chapter 16

The next day, with a steaming chicken pot pie in hand, Tessa knocked on Mr. Flatts' front door. Within a minute, he answered, dressed in wrinkled khaki pants and a white T-shirt, far from the put-together outfits he wore to the community outings.

"Tessa, how are you, dear?" he said, looking down at his scruffy attire. "I wasn't expecting anyone today. Don't mind my attire."

She assured him that he looked fine and that she was well, and he ushered her in the door. "It's freezing out their today. Can't let all that cold air in here. It takes the heat too long to bring the temperature back up."

Tessa sidestepped so he could firmly shut and lock the door. "I wanted to bring this over to you for lunch. You mentioned the other day that you loved my nana's recipe. I'm not making any promises that it's as good as hers, but I did follow her steps as closely as I could."

Mr. Flatts lifted the tinfoil that was covering the pie, sending a jet of steam toward his nose. He inhaled deeply and smiled. "Smells just like your Nana's, I'll tell you that. Come in, we can have a piece together."

"No, no, I wasn't trying to intrude. I wanted you to have it as a thank-you for inviting me down to help out with the pageant yesterday. I forgot how lovely it was."

Mr. Flatts insisted. "Come sit with me, and please, I should be thanking you. There doesn't seem to be as many people in Chestnut Ridge as there used to, and it's great to have the extra hands. Let me at least get you a cup of coffee—though you are missing out on this pot pie."

"Coffee, I'll take you up on. But the pie is just for you." She followed him back to his kitchen where he lifted the pot from the brewer. She placed the chicken pot pie down on the counter and she casted a glance over the interior of the house. It was unique and inviting, just like Mr. Flatts.

"You have a beautiful home here," she said, her eyes still taking it all in.

"Thank you," he said. "Cream or sugar?"

"Believe it or not, I drink it black."

"Ah!" he said, his pointer finger in the air. "I knew I liked you. That's the only way to drink it. Can't trust those people adding all that sugar." He handed her the mug and motioned for her to sit at the kitchen table.

He pulled out a fork and knife from the drawer and a single plate, bringing them along with the pie over to the table. "This pot pie is to die for when it's steaming hot, and since I can't sell you on a slice, I'm hoping you don't mind that I eat it in front of you."

"Of course I don't mind. Dig in!" Tessa was even more pleased she'd thought to make it for him now that she could see how much he enjoyed it.

He carefully cut a perfect triangle from the pie and set it out onto his plate, the insides pouring out. Using the side of the fork, he pulled away a piece from the crusted side and scooped up some of the filling with it, bringing the bite to his mouth. He gave it two thumbs up as he swallowed it down. "You're Nana always teased me that you were supposed to finish with the crust, but I like to eat my favorite part first."

Nodding as she took a sip of coffee, Tessa could practically hear her Nana scolding him that it wasn't the proper way to eat her pie.

After another bite, Mr. Flatts looked around the house as if to examine it. "It is a beautiful home, isn't it? But I'll tell you, it's a lot of house for one old man."

"I can see that," Tessa said. "I live alone too, in a six hundred and fifty square foot apartment with tiny, old windows . . . I'm not sure what's worse. At least here you have the space."

"When you're alone, you're alone, I suppose."

By this time, Mr. Flatts had eaten most of the contents of his plate and was scraping up the sauce and bits of crumbs, careful to finish every last bit. "Well, Tess, it wasn't your Nana's but boy, was it good."

"Thank you!" she said, feeling accomplished. "And I should get going. Don't want to take up too much of your time." She took the last sip of her coffee before standing to bring it over to the sink.

When they reached the door, Tessa buttoned her jacket and wrapped the two hanging pieces of her scarf around her neck.

"Thank you for the chicken pot pie. Brings back lots of old memories with your nana."

"You're very welcome," Tessa said as she placed both hands on his shoulders in a quick embrace. "I forgot to mention that my mom and I are cooking Christmas Eve dinner tomorrow night. We're going to do it Nana's way with the seven seafood dishes, pizza, and pasta. I know it's last minute, but we'd love it if you could join us."

His eyes brightened at the invitation. "I'd love to. I go to five o'clock mass every year, but have no plans after."

"That's perfect! We were planning on starting around six."

Mr. Flatts reached for her hand, patting the top. "Thank you for the invitation."

Tessa smiled widely. "It's our pleasure."

Back in her car, she looked at her phone, still void of new messages. Going back to her text to Chase from the night before, her good feeling now dimmed. She thought he would have responded by now.

I know you're angry, but I'd love to make it up to you. Hope you consider coming by.

***

After leaving Mr. Flatts, she turned onto the highway and started toward the shopping area. With both the heat and radio blasting, she cruised at a safe speed, careful on the twists and turns of the country road. The streets of Chestnut Ridge were one thing, and though the highway was hardly much to speak of and still consisted of only two lanes in each direction, she didn't want her lack of driving skills to interfere with her plan.

Years back, as part of one of the many campaigns she'd worked on for Jay's, they promoted keepsake pieces. It was a lull between holidays, and they were using the time to show off some of the more unique offerings from the store. After engraving the inside of a loved one's wedding ring, they make it into a necklace by adding a chain, allowing the ring to lay flat against your chest so it can always be near to one's heart. Through the years, the campaigns ran together, and she had forgotten all about the idea until the day she saw the woman in the store ask for something similar. At the time, she thought it was a heartfelt gift idea, but she didn't make the connection to do something similar for her mom until she'd spent some time back home. Thinking back on that day, when she'd walked aimlessly through the stores, she realized she'd come a long way. Just a few short days ago, her priorities were so different, and now they seemed to have realigned in a much more positive manner.

Earlier in the morning while her mom was in the shower, she crept into her room and lifted the lid of her old-fashioned jewelry box. As a child, she'd loved the jewelry box and would often ask to play in her mom's room. With the antique four post bed, floor-length mirror and the jewelry box, she'd flit from one side of the room to the other, draped in costume jewelry, living out fairy tales of being a princess in faraway lands. Her imagination had always been her strongest asset, eventually leading her down the path to advertising. From a young age, she could craft stories that brought you into whatever world she'd created. It was what made her unstoppable the first few years at the firm, though now she could see how the flame of her bright ideas had faded, cranking out uninspired ideas like the one she'd presented Jay. She'd begun favoring quantity over quality at work.

But that was about to change. She hadn't quite sorted all the details, but somehow she was going to get things back on track.

When she opened the jewelry box, her nana's white gold wedding band was laying where she last remembered seeing it, in a velvet box tucked in one of the corners. She picked up the box and carefully examined it, still able to picture it on Nana's finger. When she heard the water turn off, she put the ring in her pocket and placed the velvet box back in its place before closing the lid and scurrying from the room.

As she drove along the road, she thumbed her pocket, feeling to make sure she hadn't lost the ring.

***

Posters and displays, plastered with her past ideas, greeted her when she walked into Jay's, and a perky saleswoman popped up from behind the counter, asking her if there was anything she could help her with.

"I know it's last minute, but a few years back I saw something here that I'd like to get my mom for Christmas," Tessa said, reaching into her pocket and pulling out her nana's ring.

"Certainly! Do you remember what the piece looked like?" the saleswoman said, her bracelet of keys jingling as she walked to unlock a nearby case.

"It wasn't a specific piece. If was something much more personal." Her fist was still closed around the ring.

The expression on the young girl's face dropped as she pulled the key from the lock.

Tessa laid Nana's ring on the counter. "I used to work for Jay's, kind of," she explained. "And I once saw that you could engrave the inside of a wedding band and create a necklace from it. I was wondering if I could have that done to this ring." She slid the ring across the counter. The saleswoman picked it up to examine it before laying it out on a black, felt pad.

"Hmm, I don't see why not. Usually we can engrave in the same day. Let me take it to the back and see what they say."

Feeling optimistic, Tessa thanked the saleswoman as she made her way out from behind the counter, Nana's ring in hand.

Five minutes later she returned with a sales slip, partially filled out. There was a braided, white gold chain on the felt pad next to the ring. "Looks like we can get this done for you today. Can you write down what you would like engraved here," she said, pointing to a blank line on the slip. "And then initial here that you approve the change to the ring, and sign the bottom." She never considered that her mom may not like the ring being altered, but moving forward with her plan, she sloppily looped her signature across the bottom before carefully entering each of their initials in the blank space of what was to be engraved.

The saleswoman took the slip and read over what Tessa filled in before completing another line presumably for the chain. She paused to confirm. "You can take your pick of any chain, but I think this one will look best with the style of the wedding band."

She handed the chain to Tessa, who held it up, pinching and rolling it between her fingertips. She wanted something sturdy, assuming her mom would wear this almost every day. "I think it's perfect."

"Great!" the woman chirped as she took the chain back from Tessa, laying it on the felt. "Should be about an hour or so. You can wait in the store, or I can give you a call when it's done."

Tessa explained that it was a far drive to leave and come back, and she opted to sit on the leather couches near the front of the store. One by one she watched as customers, mostly young men, walked through the doors, looking for last-minute gifts, like her. Some of them seemed to know exactly what they were looking for, while others more resembled a deer in headlights. As they walked the store, carefully peering down into the glass cases, it was clear they were all on the hunt for the perfect gift for their special someone. Many of their eyes illuminated as they described their partners to those working behind the counters, listing off little details of their preferences they'd picked up on from spending so much time together. She couldn't help but smile as the customers shouted, "That's it!" pleased with their selections, the excitement building as Jay's employees carefully wrapped the tiny boxes in flawless red-and-green packaging and topped the finished product with a bow. The customers would leave the store looking far more relaxed and self-assured that they picked something beautiful. The gleeful anticipation to give their gift was clear on their faces.

For an hour, she watched as customers of all kinds came in and experienced something similar, leaving genuinely overjoyed with their selections, a merrier step to their walk that wasn't there when they entered the store. It seemed so simple to her now as she watched it play out in front of her again and again. It was what Jay wanted to capture in his campaign—that precise moment when customers knew they chose something exceptional and walked away feeling as jolly as old St. Nick himself.

"Ms. Gee," the saleswoman called, holding up a box. "You're all set."

Tessa jumped to her feet and approached the counter. The saleswoman took the new piece from the box and laid it out on the same felt pad. There was her nana's ring, shining with a new purpose. Four sets of initials were carved into the inner lining: hers, her mom's, Nana's, and her grandfather's. Her mom could now have the things in life she loved the most—her family, forever near her heart. Her eyes were suddenly misty. "This is exactly what I wanted," and she reached for her credit card to pay.

A grin stuck with her the entire drive home, her delicately-wrapped box sitting next to her on the passenger seat. She slipped a glance in its direction, picturing her mother untangling the ribbon and paper, expecting another gift certificate, or maybe, at most, a pair of earrings. It had been longer than she cared to admit since she believed she had something truly unique to give on Christmas morning, and her mom was more than deserving of something so special.

When she pulled up the driveway, she tucked the box into her purse, not wanting her mom to catch her when she walked in and press for details of her day. Her mom was relentless when she sensed something was going on. Tessa made a mental note to send a picture to Jay—though Ben said not to reach out—with a simple message: *Thank you.*

Chapter 17

When she entered the house, her mom was in the living room surrounded by large red-and-green plastic tubs filled with Christmas decorations. Tessa yelled a greeting over the music and put her bag down on the kitchen table, her gift hidden inside, then she stepped over more boxes of ornaments and lights to get in the room by her mom.

"You're home, perfect!" Her mom said, climbing over a tub of decorations to greet her. "I figured we'd better finish up all the decorating if we're having people over for Christmas Eve dinner tomorrow. We haven't even gotten to the tree."

Tessa looked over at the bare tree in its stand in the corner, fully opened, but without a single ornament or light. "We always did the tree late—you like it that way."

"That is true, I do like doing it last," she said, fumbling with a string of lights. "Have you heard from Chase?"

When Tessa didn't answer, her mom shook her head in understanding. "He'll get back to you eventually," And she handed over a nutcracker to place on the mantel above the fireplace. There was a tiny wooden soldier for every year Tessa lived at home, and a few for since then also. It was a tradition her mom started the year she was born. Each December, she bought a nutcracker that represented something significant from the year, or as Tessa grew and had her own opinions, it might have just been one she happened to like in the store. As soon as the Thanksgiving leftovers were packed away in the refrigerator, Tessa had an eye out for a new nutcracker. She never wanted to pick the first one that caught her attention, in case she saw something better as they did their Christmas shopping throughout the season. The tradition was the tradition—one nutcracker a year, no more, no matter what.

"Did you try giving him a call or just a silly text message? I'm surprised you younger kids can still have a face-to-face conversation after all the time you spend looking down at your phones."

"No one calls each other anymore. I'd look desperate," Tessa said, leaning over the tub to pick up one of her favorites, though it was hard to choose—each came with its own special meaning. The one in her hand was much simpler than the others, but it was larger in stature. Each year, she'd take it from the shelf, put on her ballet slippers, and twirl around the living room under the twinkling lights of the Christmas tree, pretending she was Clara from *The Nutcracker.* She'd toss her slipper at an imaginary Mouse King and save her prince, then pirouette while holding the soldier close to her chest, victoriously leaping around the room. Doing a single spin toward the fireplace for old times' sake, she put the nutcracker in its place, centered on the mantel.

After applauding her spin, her mom moved back to the subject of Chase. "It's tricky, Tess. If you're looking to just apologize for what you did, then I'd say leave it at a text. You said you were sorry. But if you want to make up with him, like *really* make up with him, then I think you might have to try a little harder. Texts can be so impersonal; the meaning behind the words can get lost."

Her mom was right—the problem was that she didn't know the exact words she wanted to say. Through text, you might lose the personal touch, but you could also hide behind the typed words. She felt bad for the way she'd yelled at him after the party, and worse for her choice of words. Before speaking to Ben, she'd been having a wonderful time. Part of her could even see a future for herself in that kind of life with Chase. But what exactly did she want from him? Her realistic side knew—she couldn't possibly expect them to simply ride off into the sunset after ten years.

"I guess, therein lies the problem. I don't know exactly what I want from him. The past few days have felt like we were never apart. You should've seen us at the party! I was having a great time—probably too good of a time with him, considering our past. If things had happened differently, we might have even kissed. But then I got that text, and I felt like I couldn't just change who I am. My job, my life—they're not here. We could never work."

With a tilt of her head, her mom placed a hand on her cheek. "You have to make the best decision for you, sweetie, but you can't expect Chase to always be there for you to fall back on.

Both of you are getting older. If you think he's the one for you, then you should tell him so. Figure out the details after."

"Pshh!" Tessa swatted her mom's hand. "That's horrible advice. Drop a bombshell like, 'I want to be with you,' with no plan whatsoever? That's a recipe for disaster. One of us will end up hurt." Her heart knew what it wanted, but there were so many other obstacles. Chase had a life in Chestnut Ridge, a thriving business, and he couldn't pick up and leave. Nor would he want to. And her life was two hours away in New York City, where there was no need for custom-built, four-bedroom, three-bath homes.

"Think about it, Tessy. There's nothing wrong with figuring it out as you go. Not everything in life can be planned." Her mom turned back to the plastic tubs and pushed a large one in her direction. "Now, get decorating. I still have to go to the food store tonight to get everything we need to cook tomorrow." Her mom jumped up, startling her. "Ah! See, you distracted me and I almost forgot!" Her mom rushed from the room to return with an unwrapped box that she handed to Tess.

"Oh, mom!" She laughed and pulled a brand new nutcracker from the box. It was dressed in a checkered apron and was holding a wooden spoon and mixing bowl.

"I figured that since you now have some marvelous skills in the kitchen, it would be an appropriate choice for this year."

Choking up a bit, Tessa said, "It's perfect." *Don't forget to stop and smell the cooking,* her Nana's letter had said. It was as if she was standing right there in the room with them.

Over the next hour they pulled item after item from the tubs and placed them throughout the house. With most of the decorations up, the ceramic Christmas village assembled and plugged in, they had everything complete but the tree. The house had transformed into a winter wonderland, with cheery décor placed in every available spot.

Moving on to the tree, they looped strands of white lights around the branches, only having to stop and replace a bulb once—a miracle in itself. One by one, they hung the ornaments. The assortment included everything from mirrored balls to weathered drawings and baby pictures, to Santa lying on beaches of their vacation destinations. They paused only to ogle over the baby photos and Tessa's handmaid ornaments from early grades in school. It couldn't be ignored—the tree was a hodgepodge of their life, from the time Tessa was born, straight through to a white-glass bulb with a painting of Chestnut Ridge on it that was a leftover favor from the holiday dinner this year.

They stepped back, satisfied with their work, then returned to the kitchen to carefully go through the pages of Nana's recipe book to make a list of the ingredients needed for their Christmas Eve feast. After a dinner of Chinese takeout—it was a house rule: no cooking the night before if you had a full day in the kitchen the next day—Tessa got ready for bed and kissed her mom goodnight before heading to her room. She plugged her phone into the charger on the wall and was changing into her pajamas when she heard it buzz against her bedside table. With her shirt still over her head, she tripped over to the phone's wire and picked it up without seeing the caller.

"Hello," she said, out of breath as she pulled her head through the collar of her shirt.

"Jeez, Tessa, you just run a marathon or something?" Ben spat on the other side of the line.

Disappointed to hear his voice and not Chase's, she pulled the flannel shirt down over her neck and pushed her arms through, alternating the phone between each hand. "Sorry, just rushed to pick up the call."

Ben mumbled something on the other end, clearly having had a cocktail or two. "Change of plans—I need you to come back to the city tomorrow. I know I said you were on a mandatory leave, but Jay is hosting an event down at the Manhattan store and he needs all hands on deck. It runs from 11:00 a.m. to 9:00

p.m. You know the address, right? It's the one near the department store."

The color drained from her face as she fumbled to press the home button on her phone, showing the date, though she already knew—tomorrow was Christmas Eve, and she had promised her mom they'd cook a perfect feast. Mr. Flatts already said he'd join them, and Chase could still say yes. "Sorry, Ben, I can't make it. Tomorrow's Christmas Eve. I have plans with my family."

"Since when do you care about plans with family?" he barked.

"Since I was told that I was cold in front of a room full of people, and you demanded I take off to find the magic in Christmas."

Noticing a trend, Ben seemed to change his mind based solely on what worked best for him. "I don't want to pull this card with you Tess. You've been a great employee, but I'm the one who said you needed the time off, and now I'm the one who's telling you that you need to come back and work this event. If we lose this client, that could mean big changes at the firm. Without Jay's retainer, we'd probably need to do cutbacks starting at the top—" He paused as if he was trying to decide if he should say what he was going to say next. "I don't want to threaten you here, but the client being on the fence with us is partially your fault. I need you back in the city, and that's final."

"But, Ben," Tessa began to argue, but he wouldn't have it.

"I'm telling Jay you'll be there at eleven, in red and green with your cheeriest Christmas smile."

"Ben . . . " Sitting down, she could feel the stress building under her skin. There was no way she could back out on the dinner she was planning with her mom—she'd be heartbroken.

"Find a way to make it there," he finished before hanging up the call.

Staring down at the phone in her hand, she felt as if it had slapped her in the face, shaking her back to reality from the world she was in. Ben hung up without even giving her a chance to convince him to reconsider, or at least hear her out. Now more than ever, she felt her job was in jeopardy. After all the years of never saying no and the countless late hours, Ben tells her to leave her family on Christmas Eve, without any consideration for her life or plans.

"Ugh!" she yelled into her pillow, hoping her mom wouldn't hear down the hall.

She forced the plug back into the phone to charge, and for the first time since she'd come to Chestnut Ridge, she set her alarm for 6:00 a.m. before pulling herself under the covers. Her mom would be devastated if she cancelled on her now—the table was already set with the Christmas china in the dining room. What if Chase decided to come and she wasn't there, having run back to the city to work a job?

Tossing back and forth, she waited for sleep to come but couldn't push the guilt she was feeling from her mind. Frustrated about her predicament, she threw off the covers and searched with her feet for the slippers next to her bed.

Once downstairs she opened the recipe book and pulled Nana's note from where it was tucked in the pages, bringing it with her to the living room where the Christmas tree stood. Fumbling behind the tree for the cord, she plugged in the lights and watched as the ornaments sent glistening colors across the otherwise dark walls. Note in hand, she sat with her legs crossed in front of the tree. As she read the note over, Nana's words, *stop and smell the cooking,* repeated in her head. Nana was right—for years, Tessa had worked toward the next project, the next meeting, giving one hundred percent of her focus to beating out a colleague for a promotion. Forget stopping to smell the cooking, she'd hardly stopped to cook at all. That first day back in Chestnut Ridge, she was a shell of the person she wanted to be—so much of the joy she'd felt over the past week had been void from her life back then. So busy with work, she hadn't bothered coming home for Christmas in years, and her relationship with her mom paid the price for it. Being back made her realize just how lonely her mom must've been—how she was lonely too. Tonight, as they hung the ornaments, she couldn't help but notice that a majority of the decorations looked like they hadn't been pulled from the attic in a long time . . . probably not since Nana passed.

As she watched the lights dance across the walls, she realized she didn't want to leave Chestnut Ridge for an event with a client. A client whose advice directly contradicted what she was now being asked to do—leave her family, everything that was important, to get back to the grind of work. Sitting in front of the tree, she knew she didn't want to be the girl alone in her apartment. She wanted to cook Christmas Eve dinner with her mom. She wanted Chase to see she was so much more than her job. When Nana passed, she made a whole list of promises that had been left undone, and she couldn't let the same thing happen again. There was no price for time spent with family—it's one of the few things money couldn't buy.

Folding the letter back in half, she kissed the outside and held it to her chest. "I'm going to stop and smell the cooking, Nana. I promise."

Back up in her room, she reached for her phone before she lost her nerve and typed her first e-mail in a week. She told Ben she would not make it into the city tomorrow and that she would be happy to return to the office as planned in January. She stated that if the decision to stay with her family for Christmas Eve was going to cost her the job, to please consider this her two weeks' notice. Without even a second read, she pressed the send button and watched as the mail icon zipped away sending the message off to cyberspace.

As the icon disappeared, her instinct was to follow up with an apology e-mail to Ben, claiming a lapse of judgement and a promise to be on the first train to New York the following morning. But she looked down at the note from Nana once more and pulled in a deep breath, then she let out a slow, drawn-out exhale, reassuring herself she was making the right call. The e-mail was sent, the decision made, and she trusted the consequences would play out as they were meant to.

Life was short, and she owed it to her mom to spend Christmas together. Not only was she going to cook up an amazing meal the next day, but she was going to take a pause and appreciate the ones around her and enjoy her holiday at home with family. If she could convince Chase to come, that would be the icing on a long-overdue piece of cake.

Chapter 18

By seven the next morning, Tessa was up, dressed, and ready to make her Christmas miracle happen. She needed to get out early and had a few stops to make before her mom locked her up in the kitchen breading the fish.

Scribbling out a quick note on the counter that she would pick up breakfast, she unhooked the keys from the ring by the door, bundled in her jacket, hat, and scarf, and was on her way. Once in town, she waited patiently for the drugstore to open and took her time reading over the holiday cards in the seasonal section. Not only was she looking for something beautiful, but she was hoping to find the words she couldn't come up with herself. Her eyes browsed the labels that topped each section, one catching her attention: *Wish You Were Here.* Tessa flipped through the cards, skipping over many with messaging that referred to something more somber and finally landing on a simple red card with a wrapped present on the front placed under a tree.

The tree is filled with lights. The presents topped with bows.

Santa's in his sleigh, but I miss you so.

The turkey's in the oven. The house is filled with cheer.

But Christmas won't be Christmas without you here.

Grabbing the gold envelope from the shelf, she picked up a poinsettia from a nearby table and signaled to the cashier who was fiddling around in the window display that she was ready to pay. Once handed her change, she asked if she could borrow a pen that the cashier cautiously handed over, as if it was a high-priced item she would run out of the store with. Addressing the top of the card to Chase, she crossed out "turkey's" and replaced it with "seafood's," underlined "without you here," and wrote out her own note underneath the poem in her near-perfect penmanship:

I'm ready to concentrate on who I am, and not what I am. I think you might be surprised. This one was always my favorite of us. Hope to see you tonight.

Reaching into her purse, she pulled out the faded picture she'd kept in the box under her bed. Placing it inside the card, she stuffed both into the envelope, then sealed it. She wrote, "Please Read" on the outside.

The pit in her stomach grew as she drove to Chase's house. What if he was outside shoveling snow or had someone visiting? Grand gestures were not familiar to her, mostly due to the fact that she secretly lacked the confidence to pull them off. Stopping out front without pulling in the driveway, she picked up the poinsettia off the passenger seat and collected herself before slipping out of the car and up to his front door. Days ago, she mocked people who stopped over at neighbor's houses, but after a week in Chestnut Ridge, she was already on her third drop-in.

When she got to the door, she raised her hand to knock but lost her nerve, feeling desperate and like a fool all at once. Spinning on her boots, she rushed down the stairs and made it halfway down the path before she heard the door unlock behind her.

She stopped dead in the snow, reluctant to turn back.

"Playing a little holiday ding dong ditch, are we?" Chase asked, holding a cup of coffee and still wearing only a T-shirt and his flannel pajama pants.

Smiling sheepishly, she turned. "Technically, I didn't ring the doorbell."

"Technically, no. But you did come up onto my porch and think about it."

With a roll of her eyes in his direction, she walked back up the steps. "I have a present for you, but was undecided where I should leave it." She switched her glance down to his pajama pants. "And I was wondering if I should've called first."

Chase put his coffee mug down on the porch railing and took the poinsettia from Tessa's arms. "You're bringing me flowers now?" She hoped his smirk meant he didn't think it was lame.

"It's what people do at Christmas—exchange poinsettias, ornaments, any holiday token really."

Biting his lip and shaking his head, he reached for the card.

"Wait!" Tessa said, skipping a step to reach him before he lifted the seal. "I don't want you to read it while I'm here."

From the top of the porch, he looked down at her with a curious stare and a spark of deviancy, clearly wanting to break her rule. She pleaded with her eyes, mouthing *please,* and began to slowly back down the porch steps. With two feet secure on the slushy pavement, she exhaled. "Thank you."

He yelled, "Merry Christmas," as she gracelessly made her way back to the car. Pausing to look back briefly, Chase lifted his hand to a full-palm wave before going back into the house, his arm hooked around the poinsettia, coffee in hand.

Tessa closed her eyes, wishing out loud that she would see him tonight before switching the gear into drive. She had one more stop to make.

At the local fish market—a small shack of a shop off the beaten path—she placed a request for the staff to cut and clean fresh calamari. She purposely left off the dish when making the grocery list with her mom so she could surprise her last minute. The man behind the counter handed her the brown paper package. The quaintness of shopping small, without the hoards that filled the organic shops in the city, delighted her.

Her last stop was the bakery where she wanted to pick up her mom's favorite sour cream doughnuts and two large cups of hazelnut coffee for breakfast. Sticking to Nana's rule to always choose take-out for other meals on days you're cooking for many. *No matter how well you plan, it always takes longer than you think,* she'd say as she'd bite off a piece of an Italian submarine sandwich mere hours before presenting her guests with an exquisite homemade meal.

The bell sound from her phone signaled a voicemail, and Ben's name popped up on the screen. The beating in her chest picked up its pace. *Was he calling to say that he accepts her two weeks' notice?* She thumbed the notification left to clear the message, uninterested in Ben's explanation for now. Whatever news he brought, it would be the same after Christmas. There was nothing he could say to her now that would change her mind. When her phone rang again, she reached to press ignore but saw it was her mom calling to ask where she was.

"I left a note. I ran out to grab some breakfast before the shops closed for Christmas Eve."

Her mom sounded relieved. "I thought you were bailing on me, hoofing it back to the city to get out of doing all this cooking you planned."

She rounded the corner to their house and let her mom know she was down the street. "Sorry, Mom, but you're stuck with me this year."

"Good, then get that cute tush of yours home and into your apron. These seven fishes aren't going to cook themselves."

When she pulled up to her house, brushed with a new dusting of snow, the worry of her future faded. She was home.

Chapter 19

Eventually, after three voicemails, Tessa caved and answered Ben's call just before nine in the morning. After a fiery, one-sided conversation and a last-minute threat that if she wasn't on her way back to the city in the next half hour to make it to Jay's 11:00 a.m. event, he'd have to let her go, she'd had enough.

"I stand by my e-mail. It's not possible for me to get to the city today. Not after all the years that I never said no, all the times I put the job first, and the Christmases and special events I've missed with my family. If you're going to make me choose between my job and staying in Chestnut Ridge, then I've made my choice. I'm staying in Chestnut Ridge for Christmas." Her confidence in the decision grew the more he fought her on it.

There was a frustrated, quiet tension between the two of them. "I don't want to have to do this, Tess. But I need you here in New York. You know having Jay's as a client is vital for this firm. We're in save mode here—it's a priority."

"I know all of this, and I won't make you say it." She'd made her decision and she would stand by it. "I put in my two weeks' notice last night over e-mail. All you have to do is accept my resignation."

Pushed to his limit, Ben let out a defeated sigh. "You're really going to throw all this away? Your career, your life, everything you've worked so hard for . . . over a Christmas dinner in the country?"

But Tessa didn't see it that way. After the days she'd spent at home learning to decompress, and the note from Nana, she'd realized that there were so many things missing from her life. It was getting harder to ignore. Because of the job and the hours that came with it, she'd lost time to do everything else. Sure, she felt accomplished—she'd built herself from a college graduate to an executive in eight years—but she had lost friends and family along the way. Her love life revolved around casual dates with men equally or more driven than her, and nights alone, watching endless hours of Netflix with a glass of wine. But most importantly, she'd lost years of invaluable time with her family. She didn't want to miss out on the time she had left with her mom, like she had with Nana.

Being home, back in Chestnut Ridge—the town she'd so desperately tried to escape—it was easy to see that she would happily trade her job and salary without a thought in exchange for one more homemade meal with Nana. As Nana said, there was always another job, but there wasn't always time to make another memory with the ones you loved. She missed the opportunity to make new memories with Nana, and all she could do was hold onto the ones that she had. But she still had time with her mom and with Chase. Sometimes in life, it is better late than never.

"I'm sorry, Ben. I really am. But you were the first to say it after I blew the meeting with Jay. I didn't see it then, but it's clear now. I'm burnt out—I've overdone it for too long, and everything in my life was suffering because of that, even my work at the firm. I need some time away from things to figure out what I want and what I'm going to do next." She looked down at her watch and realized the conversation had already gone well over fifteen minutes, and it was likely that her mom was beginning to wonder about her down in the kitchen. "I have to go. I'm sorry. Have a Merry Christmas."

She hung up the phone feeling relieved, though her hand still shook with a slight tremor, her anxiety undeniable with the magnitude of the decision she just made. There would be plenty of time to agonize over whether she made the right choice, but today she had her family, and that was enough to make her confident in her decision.

Down in the kitchen, her mom looked up from the counter, her hands busy forming crab cakes from the mixture of crab, vegetables, breadcrumbs, and egg. "Everything alright, sweetie?" She slapped a freshly-formed patty onto the baking sheet.

Tessa unhooked her apron from over the back of the kitchen chair and tied it around her waist. "Yes and no . . . I just quit my job." Her mom's eyes snapped to attention. "Please don't freak out—I actually have a lot in savings, and I can always find something new. I just . . ."

312

Her mom's concern faded into a smile. Wrapping her arms around Tessa's neck, her hands flexed, careful to not get the crab mixture on her back. "Honey, you don't have to try to convince me. I think this is great news."

Tessa couldn't help but laugh. "Seriously, aren't you supposed to tell me to be responsible or something? That I have bills, expenses, and I can't just walk away from my paycheck? That I need to act like an adult?"

Hushing her, she said, "You've been acting like an adult since you were eight years old. I think a little spontaneity is long overdue."

With a grin, Tessa dug her hands into the bowl and formed a small patty in her palm, then carefully flipped it onto the pan. "Ben wanted me to go to an event today in New York. Pretty much gave me an ultimatum. Said it might cost me my job if I didn't go. I e-mailed him late last night that if that was the case, to consider that my notice. Part of me was hoping he'd say, "Don't be ridiculous. See you after the holiday." But that wasn't the case. I really do think things happen for a reason, though."

Her mom assured her she made the right choice. "It's Christmas Eve! How could he even have the nerve to ask you to leave your family to go to some silly event? Christmas is a time meant for family. Not clients."

Tessa knew how he had the nerve. Because he had asked many times before, and the answer had always been yes. "He's so used to me doing what needs to be done, no matter what day it is. I just felt different this time. I was tired of giving everything else up." She scraped the sides of the bowls to get enough mixture to form the final patty. With the crab cakes done, Tessa rinsed her hands under the faucet. "I didn't know if I should tell you, but Nana left me a note in her recipe book. Part of it said that I should remember to take some time to stop and smell the cooking. It really stuck with me. For so long I've been go, go, go. The timing just felt right to pause and take a break, figure out what's next."

Her mom followed her to the sink, pumping soap into her hands with her wrist. "I knew about the letter. I didn't read it and she never told me what it said, but I knew she put it in the recipe book for you to find."

Tessa dried her hands with a towel. "Nana just had a way of making you see things clearly. I read it the night we got in our fight—the night I came home from the party. I was feeling so low. I had just yelled at Chase and fought with you, and then like magic, there it was for me in the exact moment that I needed to hear it. And it just made so much sense."

"Your Nana loved you very, very much. And she was a smart little lady. You learn a lot in a long life like hers."

Tessa nodded in agreement. "So, anyways," she paused to laugh. "I'm unemployed."

"Yes, you are, but let's not worry about that now. There won't be any cooking for you to stop and smell if we don't get on it. This kitchen needs to kick into high gear—we've only done the crab cakes. That leaves six more fish dishes and the pasta sauce. I figured we'd make the pizza together tonight after everyone gets here, just like we used to."

Tessa looked down at the list on the counter. They still had to wrap the scallops in bacon, peel the shrimp, and shuck the clams for the Clams Oreganata. The mussels were easy; they'd drop them in the spare sauce once it was made. That left the cod filets and the calamari. "I have a surprise for you."

"Oh yeah?" Her mom's head tipped with interest.

Tessa opened the refrigerator door and pulled out the brown package. "It has to be done last so they don't get tough, but I had the fish market clean and cut us some calamari. I know it's your favorite, and I think I remember how Nana used to make it. I thought we'd give it a try."

Her mom's eyes filled with tears, and her face shone with a bright smile mixed with both joy and sadness. "Oh, Tessy, I love you. I'm so happy you're home."

Chapter 20

The refrigerator was filled with trays of prepared food waiting to be cooked in the oven. After the crab cakes, her mom pulled out the largest sauce pot she had. Red sauce was needed for more than one dish—they needed to make enough for the pasta and the mussels, to top the pizza, and to serve on the side of the calamari. Tessa handed her mom jar after jar of preserved tomatoes from the garden that had been blanched and stored for this exact occasion. No matter how successful of a crop they'd have of fresh Jersey tomatoes, it was never enough to fill the large sauce pot. They'd always had to fill in with cans of store-bought diced or pureed tomatoes, but could proudly still taste the homegrown flavor.

Tessa stirred as the tomatoes bubbled into a delicious sauce, careful not to let it sit and burn, sprinkling spices and a touch of an Italian red wine along the way to enrich its taste. On the stove burner next to the sauce, her mom carefully fried up thin pieces of cod to a perfect golden brown. They'd had been battered in Nana's unique crust of parmesan cheese, garlic, and smashed up Ritz crackers. Later they'd reheat the lightly-fried fish in a lemon and white wine sauce before serving it with the main course.

Between the steps in the recipes, they'd stop to dance to Christmas carols, holding up their wooden spoons as microphones and belting out the tunes. Tessa mocked her mom's favorite dance move, an arm roll that looked like it belonged in a Latin ballroom dance, her mom belly laughing in a way she hadn't seen in some time.

"How come Nana's scallops in bacon always tasted better than any others I've had?" she asked as she pulled the raw bacon strips from the packaging, placing them on a tray.

Her mom pointed down at the recipe in the book. "Cause Nana always added something a little special to her recipes. No fancy New York caterer is going to do that. They don't have time to put in that extra bit of love."

Tessa looked to where her mom's finger was pointed and saw the secret ingredient. Nana rolled the scallops in dark molasses before wrapping them up in the raw bacon, creating a caramelized, bittersweet layer in between the fish and the salty meat. "She really had her way of making things unique to her, didn't she?"

"Yes, she did," her mom said, pushing a toothpick through the thick scallop to secure the bacon wrapped around it. "That's how she liked it. She always tried to add something unique, give it her own twist, that way everyone would talk and wonder what she did to make her dishes that much better. You know she liked nothing more than to have an edge on people, especially when it came to her food."

With the trays of scallops now secure in the fridge and the shrimp cooked and assembled to be served as shrimp cocktail, the meal was almost complete. The clams were stuffed and ready to go in the oven, and the mussels scrubbed clean, waiting to be cooked in their own pot of sauce with the addition of red pepper flakes. They needed to cook closer to when the guests were due to arrive.

"The only thing left is the calamari. Then we sit and wait until it all goes in." Her mom brushed her hands on her apron, pleased with where they were at with their preparation.

Tessa poured buttermilk into a large bowl and squeezed the juice of a lemon into it. She then smashed five cloves of raw garlic with the back of her knife and plopped them into the liquid. Unwrapping the string, she opened the brown packaging and dumped the squid rings into the bowl and covered it with plastic wrap. "They only need about a minute in the oil, so we'll leave them in the brine for now."

Her mom had the pot ready on the stove. "I don't know why I always thought this recipe was so hard."

"Nana probably wanted you to believe that so she could always be the one to make it for you. I don't think she wanted you to be able to make it for yourself. You said it, she loved an edge."

Her mom took a quick glance at a photo hanging on the wall of her with her Nana. "You're probably right—she wanted it to be something special that only she could do for me."

Tessa looked at the clock. It was only three in the afternoon. "So what do we do now? I told everyone to come at six."

Her mom pulled a bottle of champagne from the refrigerator and took out two glasses. Popping the cork well into the air like they did in the movies, she scrambled to get the glass underneath so none of the champagne was wasted on the floor. "I say we celebrate a job well done in the kitchen."

She handed Tessa a glass, raising hers in the air. "A toast!"

"The guests aren't even here yet!"

But her mom shushed her. "We'll do another one later. This one's just for me and my girl. To the most magical Christmas we have ever had together. And to what's going to be an amazing Christmas Eve feast!"

"And to Nana!" Tessa added, clinking her glass with her mom's.

"To Nana and her wonderful homemade recipes that brought us back together." They clinked glasses again, then they each took a long sip.

"Woo! I needed that after all this cooking," Tessa said, taking a second sip.

Her mom concurred, swallowing her champagne. "Have you heard from Chase?"

Shaking her head no, Tessa walked over to where her phone was plugged in to charge on the counter. "Think he'll just show up, or do you think he would call first?" At this point, she was hoping he might just show up since it didn't seem like she would be getting a call.

Her mom shrugged. "Who knows with men. You can never tell what they're thinking or what they'll do. They run on their own sets of rules, I'll tell you that much."

Tessa took up her mom's offer to put up their feet and sit for a bit and followed her over to the couch with the champagne bottle in hand. Powering on the television, the cartoon version of *How The Grinch Stole Christmas* was playing and had just started from the beginning.

"Perfect timing!" Her topped off their glasses with more champagne. "We'll take a short break. What's this movie, a half hour or so? Then we'll be back at it in the kitchen for the final touches."

Singing along to the opening song, "You're a mean one, Mr. Grinch," she poked Tessa in the arm when singing the word "Grinch." They both burst into a fit of laughter, partially aided by the glasses of champagne at three in the afternoon.

"Are you ever going to let me forget that a client called me cold? I should have never told you," Tessa said through heaving breaths.

"Never, Tessy the Grinch. Never."

Sitting back to watch the rest of the show, her stomach sore from laughing so hard, Tessa thought about how something that felt so terrible just a few days ago could now send her to pieces. When Jay had called her cold, it felt like the end of the world, but now, just days later, it felt like an early Christmas present. He had given her the gift of examining herself and her life. If he would've loved her proposal, she'd be tucked away in her stuffy apartment, alone and ordering from one of the few take-out options that stayed open on Christmas Eve. For once, it felt like everything had happened for a reason. She looked down at her feet, toasty in a pair of fuzzy Christmas socks her mom had given her for the occasion, and fluttered them in anticipation. This was going to be the best Christmas yet, she was sure of it.

Chapter 21

Chase still hadn't reached out, though it was half past five. She texted him earlier in the day to confirm the time they'd planned to start dinner, but she didn't receive a response. It was becoming more and more likely that he wasn't going to show.

Her mom gasped when she walked in the kitchen. "You look stunning!"

Feeling self-conscious, the color rose to her cheeks. "Are you sure I don't look like I'm trying too hard?" She looked down at her simple but classic red dress with a boat neck neckline. It wasn't tight, but it pulled in at the most flattering part above her waist.

Kissing Tessa's cheek and spinning her around, her mom said, "Absolutely not. You look beautiful."

The table was set, food ready for the oven, and the lights on the tree were lit. Everything was in place for a perfect Christmas Eve dinner . . . now all she had to do was wait. At a quarter past six, Mr. Flatts arrived, looking charming in a green plaid vest and his newsboy cap. He brought with him a bottle of wine and a bouquet of flowers that her mom arranged in a vase.

"Can't show up empty-handed, and I knew you two had the food covered. Not that I would've wanted to cook. Nothing I can make could've stood next to your fine cooking," he said, eyeing what was out on the counter.

As her mom poured Mr. Flatts a glass of wine, Tessa ducked into the living room to check, once again, if Chase had reached out to her. A sinking feeling came over her when she saw the blank screen, void of messages. It was possible she had been overly optimistic to think that just because she invited him, he would come. She had hurt Chase more than once, and she didn't blame him for guarding his heart.

The disappointment was visible on her face when she returned to the kitchen, though she tried to brush off the questioning from her mom, saying that she was fine and that they should move on with dinner.

"Still nothing from Chase?" her mom asked, with a quick glance at the clock.

"I don't think he's going to come. Let's just start making the pizza," Tessa said, joining them at the counter. "I probably should have assumed since he didn't respond to my invitation. I was just hoping he'd surprise me."

"It's still early," Mr. Flatts said. "Men tend to be a little behind the ball sometimes. Sometimes we don't know what's best for us."

"Psh! Sometimes? I'm sure you meant, men are *always* behind the ball," her mom joked.

"Let's not let it ruin anything," Tessa said, dropping a handful of flour on the counter top and spreading a light dusting so the dough wouldn't stick. "We'll make the pizza, then while it's cooking, we can snack on some shrimp cocktail and calamari. Sound good to everyone?"

All agreed, Mr. Flatts being the most excited for homemade pizza.

"Where'd my music go? You can't make pizza without music!" her mom yelled as she aggressively tapped her iPad, trying to pull up the account with her music. Tessa knew she was looking for the classic, "Dominick The Donkey." It was an old joke; they'd play the song and kiss their fingers to the air while pretending to be Neapolitan pizza makers.

"Did you check the volume?" Tessa asked. "Last time you said it was broken it was just muted." Sure enough, when she pressed the mute button, the Italian backbeat blasted through the speakers, causing all three of them to jump.

Her mom rolled out the homemade pizza dough and laid it on a large, circular pizza stone and added a scoop of sauce and a hefty handful of mozzarella cheese. "Now for the toppings. Since there're three of us, everyone gets a third of the pie to top as they wish." She placed a tray down on the counter that contained every pizza topping imaginable—they were sliced extra thin to lay perfectly on top of the cheese. They laid out what they wanted on their third, her mom pushing her hand away and teasing that she was encroaching on her portion of the pizza pie. Tessa poked back at her saying the space was actually hers, all the while enjoying the easy banter of such a simple tradition.

When the pizza was in the oven, she poured herself a glass of wine and picked at the shrimp cocktail. They dropped the rings of calamari in the hot oil, and Mr. Flatts commented that he'd never seen it made at home. When the rings were done, they patted off the excess grease and laid them out on a tray garnished with lemon wedges.

"Now these have always been my favorite," her mom said, dipping one into the sauce she'd poured out on her plate before popping it in her mouth. "They came out perfect, Tessy! Taste just like Nana's!" Tessa smiled, though it didn't reach her eyes. It was almost 7:30 p.m. It was definite—Chase wouldn't be coming to dinner.

Sitting back in her chair, she took a sip of wine, her smile growing as she looked around the table. Despite the disappointment from Chase's absence, she hadn't felt this centered since she was younger. Looking at her mom stuffing herself with her favorite dish, and Mr. Flatts who was thrilled to be spending the holidays with a family, even if it wasn't his, she was genuinely at ease.

She poured red sauce from the gravy boat onto her plate and dragged her fork through it, soaking the calamari with sauce before taking a bite. "Wow, you weren't lying. The calamari came out fantastic."

"Watch out, Nana!" her mom yelled. "There's a new queen of the kitchen." She raised her wine glass. "A toast to my Tessy . . . For a long time, I have hoped to be in this exact moment that I'm in now. My only girl, home with me for the holidays. It feels like just yesterday I'd be getting out your PJ's, promising you that Santa only stopped for those who were sleeping. I'm so happy that your life's journey brought you back here to our home and our family. Whatever you do next, I know you'll be great. But for now, let's stuff ourselves full, drink some more wine, and enjoy the magic of Christmas." Tessa and Mr. Flatts raised their glasses, clinking in the center of the table. "Here, here!"

***

After dinner, stomachs full with food, Tessa, her mom, and Mr. Flatts sat in their living room by the Christmas tree. Her mom lit the wood that was stacked high in the fireplace, blanketing the room in a comforting heat. It was close to nine o'clock, and they were starting to wind down when the doorbell rang. Her mom waltzed to the door, twirling in the middle of the room as she walked, having a time for herself.

Tessa had kicked off her shoes and was sitting, legs stretched out in front of her on the floor with her back against the couch. When her mom came back into the room, a skip in her step and a childish grin plastered on her face, Tessa knew why. Chase appeared in the entryway just behind her, holding a bottle of wine. At first she just looked up at him from her place on the floor, not registering that he had actually shown up. She given up on the idea of a surprise visit a few hours ago.

Scrambling to get her legs out from under her, she stood awkwardly and tried to slip her feet back into her heels. Lately, it seemed he had a habit of catching her right when she let her guard down, no matter how hard she tried to plan for the opposite.

"Sorry to barge in so late. I tried giving you a call a bit ago, but there was no answer. So, after some thought" —he paused, making it seem he might have fought with the decision longer than he was letting on—"I decided to drop in." After they'd eaten pizza, she accepted he was going to blow her off and decided to leave her phone in the other room to avoid obsessively pressing the home button to check for new calls or messages. Instead, she'd missed his call and the opportunity to freshen up.

They looked at each other in silence until Mr. Flatts and her mom caught on and she extended a hand to help him from the couch. "Why don't we go start setting out the desserts and let these two catch up." She pulled him to his feet as he joked that he would need to roll out of here if she kept feeding him. The three of them had just finished dessert, but on cue, Mr. Flatts picked up on the fact that Tessa's mom wanted to give them the room.

Once they were alone, Chase walked over to Tessa and handed her the bottle. There was a large red bow taped to the neck with curled ribbons cascading down the bottle. She knew this had been done in the store, and that he wouldn't know how to curl a ribbon if his life depended on it. The gifts she'd received from him in the past were wrapped with uneven corners and scotch tape was the only decoration. Grabbing the bottle with both hands, she mumbled a quick thank-you, before placing it down on the coffee table.

"I'm sorry I'm so late. To be honest"—he pulled his eyes from hers—"I didn't know what I wanted to do, and when you didn't answer, I thought you might no longer want me here."

Tessa reached for him. "I really am sorry for how I acted the other night. I've been putting my job first for so long, I forgot what it was like to care about anything else. You didn't do anything to deserve that, and you've been nothing but nice to me since I got back to Chestnut Ridge."

Taking his hand back from hers and sliding it into his front pocket he said, "So what now? What's next? I don't know if I can start this all over again with you if you're just going to leave again."

Tessa swallowed her words and tucked her hair behind her ears. "Let's not worry about that just yet. We can talk about it later. It's Christmas Eve, and I have a fridge full of leftovers. I'm going to go out on a limb and guess that you haven't had dinner yet."

Chase laughed. "Is it that obvious? I'm really only here for the food."

"Then we better get you what you want then," she said, swatting at his stomach.

His eyes locked with hers, the lights from the Christmas tree casting a soft glow over their faces. As she relaxed into a smile, she made a silent Christmas wish that he wanted her too.

When they entered the kitchen, her mom was already ahead of them, consolidating leftovers onto trays to heat up in the oven. She waved him off as Chase insisted he didn't need all the food she was piling on the trays. "You're a growing man. You can afford to eat it."

"I'm a little older now, Ms. Gee. The only way I'm growing is out," he said, patting his center.

"Don't be silly! Must be all that construction—you look like a Hollywood actor."

Tessa agreed. Since that first encounter at the market, she'd noticed that he had aged well. Though he was only a few inches taller than her, he seemed to have filled out in all the right places. His shoulders were broader, his face more defined. Thirty looked good on him.

They sat at the table with Chase as he ate, her mom piling two more helpings onto his plate before he could convince her he was full. After clearing the dishes, she dropped a platter full of Christmas cookies in the middle of the group. Mr. Flatts happily took seconds, smiling with each bite. Tessa also allowed herself more dessert, popping a sprinkled red-and-green sugar cookie in her mouth.

Filled with dinner and sweets alike, Mr. Flatts stood, thanking her mom for the hospitality before he announced it was time for him to call it a night. After walking him out, her mom yelled down the hall that she was exhausted and was heading up to bed, leaving Tessa and Chase alone in the kitchen.

"And then there were two . . . " Tessa said. "Want to sit in the other room? I like being by the Christmas tree."

Chase agreed and they moved to the living room. They sat quietly, each staring ahead. Tessa cleared her throat and broke the silence. "I'm really happy that you decided to come tonight."

"I'm happy to have come. I have to ask again, though . . . What are we doing here?"

"Sitting by the Christmas tree," Tessa joked.

Chase narrowed his eyes. "You know what I mean. Us . . . this." He motioned between them. "I thought I could handle just being your friend for a few days while you were back in town, but I think it's going to be harder than I thought."

"It doesn't have to be hard."

"Oh yeah, and what's your plan for that?" His tone didn't sound like he believed her.

"I don't have a plan . . . I'm just saying that we don't need to make this hard. It's Christmas. We're having fun together." She knew that wasn't enough.

Chase squared his shoulders, and now they were face to face. "I don't know if it's that easy, Tessa. I loved you. I would have done anything for you back then. But you left and cut off all contact. And not once have you stopped to think about how that felt for me."

Tessa tried to stop him, but he continued. "At first I thought you needed space. It was hard, but I tried to give you that. But little by little, I realized that it wasn't just a break. That you were moving on without me. I let you go too long, and you were gone. For good."

"I'm not, though . . . I'm right here. I tried to be without you, and I realize now how unhappy I was every minute I spent trying to move on from you. I had convinced myself that you would hold me back, and I was wrong."

He stood, now looking down at her. "So that's the answer I've been waiting all these years for? You thought I would hold you back?" He shook his head, visibly upset as she jumped to her feet.

"I didn't say that I was right to think that, but you wanted the truth. I thought it was the best thing for me at the time, but it wasn't. I stopped believing that loving someone could be enough to make it work.

His words got tangled as he shook his head again, ultimately saying nothing.

"It turned me cold," she continued. "And I don't want to be like that anymore. Being back here in Chestnut Ridge—it made me see that I didn't like who I was, all alone in the city with no real friends, no family. No you . . . I want to take another shot at this Chase. I want to have a chance with you."

Sitting back on the couch, his head in his hands, Chase sat quietly. Tessa could tell he was considering her words, and her mind continued to race with ways to convince him. "I quit my job and have no real plan. But I knew it wasn't right for me anymore. I quit, Chase. I'm ready to focus on me."

No words came from his mouth, but his look was telling enough.

"It's a pretty long story," she said with a laugh, but the look on Chase's face implied she should take the time to tell it. She sat next to him on the couch and began her story.

"Right before Christmas, I had a holiday campaign due for Jay's Jewelers, and let's just say I completely missed the mark. The client was unhappy, said it lacked emotion, and my boss forced me to take some time off. Then he did a complete one-eighty on me and asked me to come back to the city for an event today. And something in me just didn't want to go—I didn't want to leave. It's not just that I had put my career first—I'm comfortable with that—but it became clear that I had given up everything else to have it. It just didn't seem right anymore." For the first time since that awful meeting, she felt she was being honest with herself. "There has to be a way to have it all. A way to have a job but not lose time with my family. Maybe have one of my own someday."

Chase placed a hand on her knee. "I don't think that's asking for too much, Tess." He pulled her closer, and she put her head on his shoulder, exhaling for what felt like the first time since she'd started her explanation. Under the sparkling lights of the tree, taking in the magic of the final minutes before Christmas, neither of them felt like there was more to say.

***

It was after eleven when Chase said he should probably go home. "You better get to bed, so Santa can come," he said.

She watched him walk toward his car from the front door, a light snow dancing around him as he moved. With a content, peaceful smile, she closed the door, leaning back against it with both eyes closed, her face radiating.

Back in the kitchen, she opened her laptop on the kitchen table and went to her work e-mail. Ignoring the many work-related items that filled her inbox, she searched for Jay's e-mail address and started a new message.

Dear Jay,

I hope you had a brilliant Christmas Eve event today at the Manhattan store with Ben's oversight. I'm sure it was a great success!

As you may have heard, I gave my notice at the firm and decided to move on to pursue other adventures. Don't worry . . . this is not an angry message, but one to say thank you. You were right in our meeting. I had forgotten the meaning of Christmas—I had lost sight of what made it magical.

I spent some time in one of your stores that day, watching your customers as they made their purchases, and I could see the moment you were trying to capture. Thanks to you, I was able to return home for the holidays and reclaim some of that magic with my own family, and it has been truly wonderful. I also recently purchased a unique gift for my mother from one of your stores, and I could say with the exact feeling you wanted to inspire.

So, I thank you for seeing something that I didn't see in myself, and I wish you the merriest of Christmases.

All the best,

Tessa Gee

Satisfied with her farewell, she clicked send and waited for the mail icon to show that it was delivered before shutting her laptop. Feeling like she was sixteen again, she ran up the stairs, blew a kiss in the direction of her mom's room, and tucked herself into bed. She may not believe in Santa, but there was a bit of Christmas magic she was hoping for the next day.

Chapter 22

Her alarm hadn't sung it's tune, but she was wide awake. Lifting her arms above her head, she chuckled through her yawn at her exaggerated stretch, feeling like she was acting out a scene in a movie. She'd never been a morning person, but her appreciation was growing for mornings such as this. Typically, she'd have to rush to the shower to start her routine and most days, by the time she got in to the office, her heart would be pumping out of her chest from the stress of simply getting there. The slower start was something she could get used to.

The blinds were drawn just enough that she could see a fresh layer of white powder on the trees and lawn with soft flurries still sprinkling from the sky. It was a picture-perfect scene for Christmas. Pulling an oversized sweater over her head, she slipped her feet into her slippers and knotted her hair before skipping down the hall and stairs to greet her mom. At seven-thirty, her mom would've already been up for an hour, sipping her coffee at the table, waiting for Tess to wake.

"Merry Christmas, Mom!" she said, skidding into the kitchen like a child.

Her mom wrapped her in a bear hug. "Merry Christmas, my love. Have I told you how happy I am that you're here?"

"Once or twice," she quipped. "But I'll say it again—I'm happy to be here too." She kissed her mom on the cheek and swiveled around her to the coffee pot.

Filling her cup to the brim with black coffee, she took a sip, though she didn't need the caffeine. She was wide awake and bursting at the seams of her Christmas pajama pants with excitement. "What should we do first?" she asked, topping off her mom's cup.

"You know the drill. Stockings first, then gifts. After that, we have our traditional Christmas morning breakfast, then who knows where the day will take us!" she said, rocking her hips as she listed the items.

They'd done it the same way for as long as Tessa could remember. Now as an adult, she could guess her mom had scheduled their Christmas morning routine this way so that, as a child, she could get to her presents first, knowing that Tessa's excitement to open gifts would overshadow the meal with her mom and Nana.

Back then, there was a rule: no leaving your bed until 8:00 a.m. But she remembered that most years she'd wake by six, anxiously pacing in her room as the clock on her nightstand ticked away the minutes. The hours passed excruciatingly slow, and when the hand would finally reach 8:00 a.m., she'd fling open the door and sprint to Nana's room like a reindeer on a runway. Nana would pretend to be sleeping still, just so Tessa would have to jump on the bed to wake her. She'd pull her down next to her in bed and say, "Give me my Christmas hug first!" Then she'd throw off the covers to go with her to get her mom.

When they'd finally spread out around the tree, Tessa would tear through her gifts, sending a flurry of glittered wrapping paper, ribbons, and bows across the living room. She'd spend time with each of the presents she'd received—even the clothes, holding them up to her and posing like a model, to which her nana and mom would *ooh and aah* as she spun around. Only after she worked her way through each gift and tired herself out from the excitement would they return to the kitchen for their traditional Christmas morning breakfast.

The meal was the same each year: scrambled eggs with cheese, toast, and bacon . . . lots of bacon. Tessa would pour out the orange juice and set the table with the three similar-but-different Christmas plates. Her plate painted with a gingerbread house, Nana's a Christmas angel, and her mom's had a snowman. The older women always claimed to not remember which was theirs, though they all new exactly which plate belonged to whom.

"Why change a good thing?" she said, leaning into her mom. "Onto the stockings, then!"

The night before, Tessa had stuffed some gifts for her mom in the stocking with her name on it, including last-minute additions of her favorite candy bar and a gift card to purchase more music on her tablet. Her mom had done the same, stuffing her stocking full with lotions, makeup, and other small items that she knew Tessa liked. Soon the living room was covered in torn wrapping paper, the gifts under the tree all opened except one. Tess was giddy as she excused herself and returned seconds later with the small box from Jay's, extending her hand toward her mom. She was overjoyed for her to open it.

Looking confused, her mom took the box from her and studied it closely in her hand. "Another gift? Tessy, you didn't have to go out and spend your money on something expensive for me. You being here this Christmas is more than enough."

"I know, Mom, but I shouldn't have missed those other years and I wanted to do something extra special to make it up to you. To show you that it's going to be different from now on," Tessa said, leading her toward the couch.

Once she was seated, her mom looked up at her. "You really didn't have to. You know I'm easy when it comes to gifts."

"I know, but I wanted to," she said with a bigger smile. "Now open it!" She couldn't hold back her excitement any longer.

Her mom carefully pulled at the corners of the paper and removed the box from the side of the wrapping without disturbing the bow taped on top. After another look toward Tessa, she opened the box and let out a gasp when she saw Nana's wedding ring shining with its original luster. The jewelry shop did a fine job cleaning it up before embellishing with their families' initials.

"What is this?" She lifted the chain, allowing the ring to fall to her palm.

Sitting down next to her mom, Tessa pointed toward the interior side of the ring so she could read off the initials. "Look inside."

Her mom flipped on her reading glasses that had been perched on top of her head, and she held the ring up close to her face before gasping again. "It's all of our initials!"

Tessa nodded and watched her mom light up from the inside out.

"Oh my goodness, that's the most beautiful idea! I've never seen anything like this!" Her mom clasped the necklace around her neck, lifting it from her chest to examine it once again. "How did you think of such a thing?"

"I wanted something special to commemorate this Christmas, and I know you never knew what to do with Nana's wedding ring. It just so happened that on one of the toughest days of my life, I watched as another woman asked for something similar, and the joy on her face when the jewelry store agreed to make it was indescribable. It was like she knew it would be the perfect gift. And I knew I wanted to give something like that to you."

Her mom let the ring fall back to her chest, and Tessa reached for it. "You're the heart of our family, so I wanted a way for you to keep us all close to your heart."

Her mom's happiness flooded her eyes as she squeezed Tessa in a tight hug. "Oh, Tessy, it's perfect!"

With her chin propped on her mom's shoulder, she laughed and her face filled with delight. If Jay could only see her now . . . he wouldn't recognize her.

Her mom pulled back and fanned both hands at her eyes. "Look at me blubbering—it's Christmas, for goodness sakes!" she said, laughing at herself. But Tessa felt it too—her eyes stinging just enough to make her aware of the happy tears gathering. It seemed that Nana had her hands in all of this—bringing her back to Chestnut Ridge so that she and her mom could grow closer again. Even bumping into Chase in the parking lot of the market seemed like more than mere coincidence. Looking at a picture of Nana hanging on the wall, she swore she saw a twinkle in her eye. Whether it be Nana or the magic of the season, things seemed to be falling into place.

"Onto breakfast?" she asked, already standing and moving toward the kitchen. Tessa followed behind, her hands clasped. She was thrilled that her mom loved her gift. If Jay needed it now, she'd know exactly the emotion to capture.

Soon, bacon was laid out on a rack over a sheet pan and placed in the oven—Nana's trick for perfect, crispy bacon—and her mom was cracking eggs in the frying pan on the stove. Though she was sure these tips were listed somewhere in Nana's recipe book, they knew how to make this breakfast by heart. Tessa pulled the Christmas glasses from the hutch in the dining room and spread out their themed plates and condiments across the table. Her mom appeared with the eggs and bread, placing each on the table before taking a seat.

As her mom spread a glob of jelly across a piece of toast, she lifted her eyes in her direction more than once, signaling that she had something to say.

"What . . ." Tessa said, knowing her mom was thinking up something in her mind.

"Oh nothing . . ."

"Mom," Tessa said, a brow raised. "Just say it, please. I know you're cooking up something in there, so spit it out."

After she finished spreading butter and jelly on her toast, she placed it on her plate. "How did things go with Chase last night? Not that I was listening, but I heard him leave after eleven. Something had to be said in all that time together."

Tessa bit into a piece of bacon, talking as she chewed. "Unfortunately, there's not much to report, though I know you're desperate for some gossip." Her mom rolled her eyes. "I told him I quit my job—that because of it, I was missing out on so much."

"*Mm-hmm*," her mom agreed, pushing for more information.

"I said that I wanted to believe I could do it all. Work for myself, but be able to spend time with my family. And maybe"— she raised her hand—"Don't get all crazy on me, but maybe one day even have a family of my own."

Squealing, her mom clapped her hands. "I'd love to be a nana!"

Tessa shook her head in her hands, though the reaction forced a smile. "First off, you could never be Nana . . . Nana is Nana. Second, I said don't get excited. I don't even have a boyfriend, let alone someone to start a family with. I just meant that I wanted it to be a possibility, and that the way my life was going, it didn't feel like one."

Clearly not listening to the logical side of her statement, her mom said, "Oh, heck! Don't get caught up in the details sweetie, I'll find something else for my perfect little grandchildren to call me. They can call me whatever they want."

A few weeks ago, she never would have allowed herself three slices of bacon at breakfast, but today she happily bit into a fourth. "Well, you'll have plenty of time to plan for that, don't you worry. Chase didn't seem convinced that I would stick around. He probably just thinks it's some sort of holiday phase. I'm not even sure if he wants to get back together."

Her mom paused from fanaticizing about grandmotherhood. "What do you want, honey? Do you want to be with Chase?"

Tessa bit her lip. She hadn't exactly come out and admitted it to herself, but yes, she did want to be back together with Chase. She'd never stopped wanting to be with Chase. All these years and distance spent away from each other, and she'd ignored what her heart always knew . . . she loved him. There was never going to be anyone else for her.

"Yes, I guess I do. I've wanted to be with Chase since I first saw him as a kid, and it doesn't seem like that's changed." Here at the table, after everything they'd been through, her heart still skipped a beat thinking of him.

Her mom reached for her hand and squeezed it. "Chase wants to be with you too. Deep down, I know it. I've watched him try to forget you for years, but it's always been obvious to me. He's been stuck on you since the tenth grade."

She flushed to a tickled pink at the thought of it, remembering a time when their relationship was simple, a time when true love seemed easy to believe in and a hint of a touch from him made her blush. "Then what do you think I should do?"

"Oh, Tessy, we've always been able to think of something, haven't we?" And they always had. Between her mom and Nana, they could solve any problem, heal any wound without an ounce of stress or even the need to question what should be done. Often, she'd envied the way they seemed to have it all figured out, but most times she'd sit back in awe as they twisted their magic, seeming to barely lift a finger as they finagled with problems until they disappeared.

Tessa's face twisted into a frown. "He seems so hurt by the way I left, not that I blame him. I want to do something big, something that proves that things will be different this time. That I'm not going to just pop up one day and leave again without an explanation."

They sat silently, forking their eggs and considering the possibilities. A natural-born planner, Tessa didn't like having problems she felt she couldn't solve.

Her mom's fork hit the table, dropping from her hand with a clatter. "I got it!"

She reminded Tessa of the first Christmas she and Chase spent together. Tessa had said she didn't want any presents— they'd only been together a few months, and she felt silly listing off items when he asked. But Chase being Chase, he persisted, asking her every day in December what was on her Christmas list. Finally, just a few days before the twenty-fifth, she said she wanted to go see the lights in New York. Until then, she had only seen them on television. Looking back, she thought about how neither of them had a driver's license, making it a much harder ask than something he could pick up at the mall or at a store in town. But Chase promised he'd figure out a way to take her to the city, and like many teenage boys, his promise fell flat when he couldn't convince either of their moms to drive them there.

So instead, Chase bought boxes of Christmas lights and brought them out by the lake, stringing them in trees, along the rocks and the benches, and creating a breathtaking scene of their simple, favorite spot. He'd brought the lights to her.

Earlier that day, she hadn't want to let on that she was disappointed about not being able to go to New York. When he called to ask if she could meet him, she bundled herself in layers and walked over to the lake. She made her way up the path, and she could see his silhouette in the dark, standing near the bench. As she approached, he clicked on the lights, illuminating the entire area with orbs of white. Combined with the reflection in the water and the gleam of the snow on the ground, there seemed to be thousands of them, though now she realized it was probably much less. Her eyes were wide and her heart danced with Chase's own version of the twinkling city lights. *If I can't take you to see the lights, I'll bring the lights to you,* he had said as he walked her through his creation, hand in hand. To this day, she has never experienced the rush of feeling so loved quite like she did then.

"How are we going to pull that off? Who knows how long that took him, and I still wouldn't be able to tell you how he plugged in all those strings of lights." Tessa couldn't help doubting her mom's plan. But her mom was already on her feet, reaching for the phone to ask Mr. Flatts if they could borrow the spare lights and generator from the community center. By the way she jumped up and down as she thanked him, whispering that it was for a secret Christmas mission for Chase, Tessa assumed he'd said yes.

Her mom hung up the phone and instructed Tessa to get ready, giddily clapping her hands. "And don't forget to text Chase to meet you tonight! But give us some time, we have a lot of work to do."

Before she could argue, her mom spun on her heel and headed for the stairs, yelling over her shoulder to leave everything on the table—she would clean up the breakfast plates later. Tessa dropped the dishes in the sink. Her mom must really be excited if she was willing to leave a messy kitchen.

Back in the living room, she searched for her phone and found it under a piece of torn wrapping paper. First she sent a simple *Merry Christmas* message with a Santa emoji, then she sent a second one asking if he wanted to meet her later that night at their favorite spot at the lake. Unlike the last time she invited him somewhere, his response was almost instant. A simple *Sure thing, Tess. Merry Christmas.* Nothing too telling, but it would do for now. He had agreed to meet. She closed her eyes, imagining him on the other side of the phone, happy when it buzzed with a message from her. She had made him wait long enough—today she would give Chase the best present she could: Her heart.

Chapter 23

Hours later, the sun dipped behind the clouds, and they had most of the lights from the community center strung up near the lake. It could be argued that Chase's had looked better, and he definitely had more lights, but for two women on a last-ditch mission, it looked pretty good. Trying to avoid any major mishaps, they tested each strand with the generator before looping it through whatever they could find and by 7:00 p.m., the fresh layer of snow sparkled like the night sky.

With their arms around one another, they took a moment to appreciate their work, noticing a strand or two that needed to be altered, and that her mom was quick to fix.

"Well, honey, now all you have to do is wait," said her mom, a hand on her back. "I gotta tell you, your nana would be so proud of you. For everything. I know that she's up there right now, smiling down on all this."

"I bet she is." Tessa looked up toward the sky, shivering slightly from having been out in the cold for some time. "Though she's probably much warmer. I bet she's watching with a steaming cup of cocoa."

"I'm proud of you too, Tess. I was always proud of you, but I'm just so happy that you're slowing down a bit. Life goes by fast and there're so many, many parts of it to enjoy. I'm not saying you shouldn't work hard and love your job, but you should just get a little bit of everything. And I think you see that now. I never wanted you to look back and feel like you missed out."

Tessa nodded, feeling more in control of her happiness than she ever had. When she read Nana's note that night after Zak's party, it became clear. She was sacrificing too much of one part of herself for another. She could never get back the moments she'd missed with Nana, or the time with her mom, but she could make sure she didn't miss anymore in the future. "I want to move back to Chestnut Ridge. I want to come back, so I can be with you."

Her mom turned, looking slightly shocked. "I didn't want to ask about that part of this plan with Chase. I thought to myself, 'I better not point out any major flaws,' but are you sure?" Her voice squeaked from excitement. "You love New York City."

"I do . . . or I did. I got to live that part of my life that I'd wanted so badly, and it was such a wonderful experience. But it's gotten old. I've gotten older, and I realize it's not about the outfits or the address or the title at your job. All of that was great, but I'm ready to move back home. I'm ready to be closer to you."

Leaping into Tessa's arms, her mom planted a kiss on the side of her head.

Tessa squeezed her back as she bounced up and down from joy. "I don't mean home, like our house, but maybe I can buy something of my own here in town."

With both hands in hers, her mom looked up with a smile brighter than the lights. "I'm so happy to hear you feel that way, Tessy. I think that's a great idea."

Her mom glanced down at her watch and quickly gathered her things from the bench. Chase was expected any minute, and her mom wanted to be clear away and back at the house before he arrived. With one last kiss on the cheek, she wished Tessa luck before sliding into the driver seat to return home. Now that she was alone, Tessa sighed and switched off the lights to wait.

***

What felt like hours was really only mere minutes, but Tessa hated waiting. Years spent in the fast-paced city of New York had thinned her patience to practically nonexistent. Without the sun, the temperature dropped even lower, sending a cool breeze across the lake and a chill down her back. She pulled her jacket tighter around her shoulders and the sleeves down over her mittens, rubbing her hands together to warm them.

Alone with her thoughts, she became increasingly worried with every passing minute that Chase wasn't going to show. She checked her phone twice before tucking it back in her pocket. *He'll show,* she thought, in an attempt to force confidence.

Tessa and her mom had to rush to complete their last-minute plan, leaving her with hardly any time to think through what she'd say to Chase when he got there. She refused to consider the possibility that he wouldn't want the same thing—she knew Chase, and she knew he loved her too. Rubbing her hands together faster, from the cold and the nerves, she cupped her hands over her mouth, blowing hot air. *It's going to be fine,* she told herself, repeating it in her mind. *It's going to work out.*

She was so caught up in her thoughts, she didn't hear Chase as he came up the path behind her, the sound of his boots must have been crunching in the snow with each step. "Can I join you?" he said, still a few feet away.

Startled, she jumped to her feet and quickly clicked on the lights with a lot less grace than she'd planned. With a popping noise, the strands livened all at once, sending light pouring over the snow and out across the lake.

"What's this?" Chase asked and stopped on the path. He was visibly shocked by the gesture. Not that either of them didn't recognize the scene, instantly brought back to years earlier when they first fell in love.

With one last deep breath, Tessa opened her mouth and spoke the words from her heart. "I never should have left you all those years ago. I loved you then, and it should have been enough to try for what we had. I chickened out, pushed you away, and spent years hiding from the fact that I still love you Chase. I've never stopped. And I think . . . or I hope that you still love me too."

Chase looked over the lights, a smile creeping slowly onto his face. "How did you do all this?"

"Well, I stole the idea," Tessa laughed. "Ripped it off this guy I know, and my mom is a great helper when she's put on the job."

Taking two steps toward her and pausing, Chase said, "I guess that guy had it coming . . . Tell me again."

"What? That my mom's a good helper?"

Now standing directly in front of her, he said, "No, the other thing you said."

"I love you, Chase. I've always loved you." Leaning in, he cupped her face in his hands and smiled before kissing her. Her entire body relaxed as she wrapped her arms around his neck.

He paused with his hands still to her face and said, "I love you too, Tessa Gee. You're the only thing I've ever wanted." And he brushed his lips across hers. The lights and flurries tunneled around them as they shared a kiss they'd both been waiting for.

Pausing one more time, he took a step back and pulled away. "How do we make this all work? I love you, and I'll try anything you ask, but I just don't see how it will work with you hours away in New York . . ."

She moved back in toward him and placed a single finger to his lips, silencing his worry. "There's one other thing . . . I'm moving back to Chestnut Ridge."

Shaking his head with an easy laugh, he said, "So that's, that? You're moving back? If you're kidding with me, that would so not be nice." She bobbed her head yes, grinning. "I never thought I'd see the day. My Tessa, moving back home to Chestnut Ridge from the big city."

To her surprise she liked the sound of that. Back in Chestnut Ridge meant back with Chase and her mom. Two people she never wanted to be away from again.

"So, no more New York?" he asked, still in disbelief.

"Well, you'll have to help me pack. Not that I have much, but getting anything into a truck in New York is a challenge." He laced his fingers through hers and told her he thought he could manage.

Obviously still shocked, it was clear there were a million thoughts running through his mind, and Chase was trying to put together the pieces of what this meant for them. He was a born problem solver, and his first thought was to offer her a job helping to manage and promote his business. Tessa said she'd consider it, then he moved onto asking where she'd live. This time, she placed her entire palm to his mouth. "We can figure it all out over time. I promise."

"So what now, then?" he asked, taking her hand in his.

"My house. Christmas dinner." She stood on the tips of her toes and kissed his cheek. Their eyes locked, and the reflection of the lights glistened on each of their faces.

"Great, I'm starving," he said, returning a kiss to her lips.

With their hands interlocked, they walked along the strands of lights, taking in the magic around them. Tessa didn't have all the answers. There was plenty to discuss. But through Nana's words, she now understood that she didn't have to have it all figured out. There were plenty of times in life that called for a solid plan and an understanding of every last detail. But sometimes, like Nana said, it was better to just stop and smell the cooking.

Looking up at the twinkling sky, she smiled, whispering a thank-you, and hoping that it would make its way to Nana. She'd come to realize that you're never too old to go home, or to believe in the magic of Christmas. She would always remember this Christmas as the time she did both . . . and her life was that much better for it.

Chapter 24

When they walked in the door back at her house, her mom rushed to meet them, and her face lit up when she saw Chase was there too. She opened her arms wide and pulled him in for a hug, squeezing and rocking as she told him how happy she was to see him back with her daughter. When she finally let him go, he turned toward Tessa. "Well, you have one heck of a daughter, Ms. Gee. I'm lucky she wants me." Her mom corrected that they were lucky to have each other.

"And I must say, that was one heck of a job on those lights. As someone who tried that stunt myself one time, I know the work that went into it." Her mom insisted that it was a piece of cake as she ushered them back into the house.

Back in the kitchen, Tessa saw that the breakfast dishes were cleaned and put away and been replaced with a beautiful Christmas setting for dinner, complete with candles and glasses for a toast. Tessa pointed out that the table was set for three.

"How were you so sure that Chase would be with me when I walked back through the door?"

"I've watched you two dance around your love for years. Enough was enough," she cried, crisscrossing her hands. "When your eyes locked on each other the night Chase picked you up for the party, I just knew the timing was finally right. You fell in love as teens, separated, lived your lives, made something of yourselves" —she paused to roll her eyes at Tessa, —"and now you're back, still in love, and ready for the next step." Neither Tessa nor Chase could argue with this version of their story.

Chase put an arm around Tessa and kissing her quickly before they all sat to eat.

"Another toast," her mom said, raising her glass. "To you two. I'm so happy you have found your way back to each other. And cheers to the best Christmas this house has seen in a long time."

After they cheered, clinking their glasses, Chase stood. "Thank you, Ms. Gee. This has been the best Christmas yet." He took a sip from his glass and placed it on the table. "And I'd like to make it even better."

He winked at Tessa and knelt on one knee, taking her hand in his. Her mom's hands covered her mouth, muffling the sound of shock. "When I saw you that day in the parking lot, I knew it was now or never. For a long time, I've wanted one more chance, and I knew that's what it was. I let you go too easy, and I hoped for a day that I could show you I never wanted to let you go again. This wasn't part of the plan tonight, so I'm embarrassingly unprepared and don't have a ring. But I promise you, not only will I buy you whatever ring you want, but I will love you unconditionally, exactly as you are, for the rest of your life, if you let me. I lost you once, and I never want to lose you again." He paused, everyone in the room hanging on his every word. "Tessa, make me the happiest man in the world this Christmas. Will you marry me?"

After all her life planning and strategizing, Tessa never could have expected she'd be where she was in this exact moment, looking down at Chase as he promised to love her for who she was, not what she could do for him, for the rest of her life. For once, instead of considering the logistics and whether things would work out exactly as she'd like, she knew she could offer him exactly the same in return. To love him for him, in his Chestnut Ridge couture flannel and all.

Emotion filled her eyes and her heart. "You're perfect for me. You always have been. Of course I'll marry you." She stood and wrapped both arms around his neck as he lifted her from the ground, spinning her in a circle before kissing her.

As she slid back down toward the ground, her mom locked her arms around them both, alternating kisses from his cheek to hers and jumbling her words from happiness. As Tessa looked from Chase to her mom, both of them grinning from ear to ear, she knew this family was something she could get used to . . . something she too would want to hold onto and never let go.

As the three of them settled down, Chase picked up Tessa's hand, kissing where a ring would have been placed. "I'm sorry I wasn't better prepared. Something just happened tonight, and I knew I didn't want to wait another minute. I want to do things right this time, Tess. From the very beginning."

Tessa laughed. "I know you're good for it," she said as he placed another kiss to her finger. "I'm not worried about the ring. It's the feeling that matters most, not the piece of jewelry. And right now, I feel like I want to spend the rest of my life with you."

Her mom had calmed down some, and officially welcomed Chase to the family before blurting out that they had so much to plan.

"So, will you work with me?" he asked. "My job offer still stands."

"I don't know about that one." She laughed. "But we'll see. I don't know what I'm going to do about a job just yet."

"But you'll move in with me?" Chase asked, with a perk of his head.

Looking at her mom, who nodded, hands clasped, she said, "That one I can do." She hugged him again, overwhelmed with all that was happening before she moved over to her mom, embracing her tight and whispering a thank-you into her ear. Her mom looked at her, then over to the picture of them and Nana hanging on the wall. It seemed things were finally as they should be.

"Tomorrow when the stores open up, we can go pick out whatever you want," Chase promised.

With a smirk, Tessa said, "I think I know just the place."

Chapter 25

Standing at the counter in the Manhattan store for Jay's Jewelers, Chase explained to the saleswoman that they were there to pick out an engagement ring for his beautiful new fiancé. When the woman realized that Tessa was his partner, she bounced up and down, cheerfully exclaiming they had come to the right place. And Tessa couldn't agree more. Chase asked where she wanted to go shopping for a ring, and she immediately said Jay's, which he happily agreed to, saying he knew of one close to Chestnut Ridge. When she corrected him, saying she had specific store in mind, he hesitated a little but gave in, taunting that he knew she'd find a way to get him to New York, one way or another.

She wanted to go back to the store she'd visited that fateful afternoon when her life seemed to be crumbling, but ultimately was building up to something even better, something she couldn't have dreamed of. Standing out front of the decorated windows, she looked at her own campaign, seeing it now in a completely new way. That day, she thought she knew what love was—she had been asked to show it time and time again in her campaigns. But after all the twists and turns this Christmas had brought her, she felt love like she never had before.

Being back in the city at that store was the fairytale ending to her own story of finding herself again back home. If not for Jay and her forced time in Chestnut Ridge, she might never have transformed from the icy princess, alone in her downtown tower, to someone who believed she could have it all. Someone who now understood that love and family were just as important as money and status. There were many steps along her path, but it all started at her bust of a meeting with Jay's.

"So, do you know what you're looking for—is there a setting or cut that you prefer?" the saleswoman asked. Chase looked to Tessa for an answer. Many times, as she'd watched colleagues and friends get engaged, she'd wondered what her own ring would look like one day. At one point she had an idea of what she might like, but today with the opportunity in front of her, she felt differently.

"Surprise me," she said, smiling up at Chase. He squeezed her tight against him.

The woman jingled away, keys rattling, and returned with multiple options laid out for her to try on. She and Chase picked up each one, looking it over before placing it back on the felt tray.

"Tessa Gee, is that you?"

Tessa turned to see Jay himself, dressed in his standard three-piece suit, standing behind her.

"Jay!" she said, meeting his hand. "What are you doing here?"

Jay laughed and looked around, holding both his hands up. "Well, it is my store."

Shaking her head, Tessa said, "Of course." She turned to Chase and said, "This is my"—she paused to smile wide—"my fiancé, Chase."

Jay's eyes flashed a knowing look as he shook Chase's hand. "Look at that! Congratulations to you both. What brings you in then?"

Chase, quick to explain, shared how it was a surprise engagement and that they were here to pick a ring.

"I think I know just the one!" Jay said, whisking past them and calling back over his shoulder to wait where they were.

He returned a few moments later with a single engagement ring in a small black box. He motioned for Chase to come over by him first, lifting the lid, to show him the ring. By the way Chase's demeanor changed, she knew it was the one.

Jay handed the box to Chase, telling him they could take care of the payment later, and Chase shook his hand. He slowly walked back over in her direction, her hands clasped tightly together at her waist, she was giddy from the anticipation.

"I know you already said yes, but let's make it official." He flipped open the box, revealing the most exquisite engagement ring she'd ever seen. The details on the setting were unlike anything she'd seen—the diamond as bright as a light on top of a Christmas tree. "Marry me," he said, sliding the ring on her finger. Speechless, she could only nod her head yes.

As Chase pulled her in for a hug, she saw Jay watching from afar. Before he turned to walk away, he winked and grinned, which she returned.

After leaving Jay's and heading back out into the city, they walked toward the apartment she'd soon be packing up. She held her hand out in front of her, admiring her new ring against the backdrop of New York. Chase once promised her he'd bring her the city lights, and in a way, he had. He allowed her to find herself, and she was more than thankful that he had—she couldn't see how they would have worked another way. As she walked the same city street she had many times before, there was a new stride to her step. She had come to New York, looking to fulfill what she thought would make her happy, and through her experience, was brought full circle, returning to the love that she already had at home. And through all that, she had *made it*, in more ways than she ever imagined she would.

This Christmas, she was given the best gift of all. She reconnected with the family of her past, and had a new hope for one in the future. She promised to never forget to slow down and enjoy a delicious meal, no matter where her life led her. Luckily, in her family's house, taking a moment to stop for a good long whiff would never be a challenge. The food always smelled great.

ABOUT THE AUTHOR

CS Jane has always loved telling stories and making delicious home-cooked meals as part of holiday traditions. *Cooking Up Christmas* is her debut holiday novel.

If you enjoyed reading *Cooking Up Christmas,* please kindly leave a review on Amazon.

Made in the USA
Monee, IL
10 June 2022

97780454R00225